Arson

....

Vincent Freul

Contents

1 Ablaze

The everyday monotony of my labor ordinarily allowed for time in which my eyes could wander. Though in this small space behind my father's bookshop, there was nothing more to view than the familiar tomes and the machinery used to print and bind them.

I observed my younger sister Liza employing the final embellishments upon a new edition before glancing back to my own work and stifling a yawn. The air within the workshop was always stiff and warm, especially so on a muggy London summer day like today.

My fingers worked nimbly at the seams, sewing the pages together as my eyes roved over the colorful artistry contained within. A book of modern art. That was the newest project that plagued us. My father had promised a veritable library of them to some rich fellow from the northwest region of London and we were on a deadline. For that reason, Liza and I had hardly slept a wink in over eighteen hours now if the clock above the press were to be believed. That fact, paired with the heat, did well to practically incapacitate us with exhaustion.

"Did you read the papers this morning?" my sister asked out of the blue. I glanced over to find that she was not looking my way. She was still working away, crafting the elegant swirling pattern which adorned so many of our family's books and was a design all her own.

"I never do," I reminded her, going along with her attempt at conversation as a method, I imagined, of keeping herself awake. "Anything interesting?"

"Some rich toff got his valuable artwork stolen."

"Pity."

I watched my little sister yawn as a clatter sounded from the room directly in front of us. Liza's eyes slid from the door to me and I could see the question there.

I rose to my feet, brushing my hands against my skirts as I did. I gave her a nod to indicate that I would see that everything was alright, doing my best to ensure her of my certainty that it was, and then I headed for the door. I entered the hallway beyond, only slightly less stifling than the workshop I had left behind, and walked swiftly to the door that led out into my father's shop. I hesitated at the threshold.

Liza and I were to remain unseen. That had always been a house rule. We were women, after all, and we did not want to offend a purchasing man's sensibilities by attempting to sell anything to him. For that reason, our skill had always been in binding and embellishment rather than salesmanship.

Another clatter from beyond the closed door spurred my feet onward and I, forgetting my propriety in the face of the strange commotion, turned the knob gently and pushed the panel open.

On the other side was my father, still standing behind his long oak counter. But a man I did not recognize, the largest, most terrifying man I had ever seen, leaned over that counter and hoisted my father completely off of his feet by his collar. I gasped before I could think better of it. The man's face snapped in my direction. He had a long, white scar over his left eye and his wicked smile widened to a toothless grin at the sight of me. He nodded a head in my direction and I saw his companion for the first time. Much smaller and lankier but no less terrifying, the man stepped out from the shadows and crossed the room in three long strides to reach me.

I turned to flee but he caught my wrist and pinned me against the wall next to the door. With lightning speed, he pulled a knife from some hidden place on his person and held it deftly at my throat. His face was inches from mine, expression carved into a sneer. I could smell the ale on his breath.

"Don't hurt her!" my father screamed. I could see him and the other man just beyond my captor's left ear. My father was still in the air, held by his collar, but his eyes were on me. I could see the utter terror within them as his round face reddened and he begged the man who held him. "Please. Don't hurt my daughter. I will do anything you ask of me. Anything. Please."

The desperation in my father's voice brought tears to my eyes but I refused to allow them to fall. I would not give these men the satisfaction in knowing that they had pained me and I had far too much pride to show them fear.

The man holding my father looked from him to me and back again, eyebrows creased in concentration. His companion removed his eyes from me to watch the man holding my father who seemed to be the leader of the two. A small sliver of light caught my attention and I turned my head slightly to see that the door I had entered through was now cracked slightly. I saw my sister's terrified eyes peering into my own through the slit. Unable to shake my head with the knife at my throat, I carefully reached out a foot and, while the men were distracted with their wordless communication, nudged the door closed on her, praying that she would stay hidden beyond or, better yet, flee from the back door and retrieve help.

"You have four days, old man," the thug growled so low that I almost couldn't hear him. Then he released my father's shirt and sent his companion a quick jerk of the head.

The lanky man released me and the two of them exited the shop. The moment they were gone, I ran to my father. He was slumped against the counter, elbows on the top, face in his hands. He was shaking. I placed my arms carefully around him and said nothing for a moment as my mind raced for an understanding of what had just occurred.

We hadn't been robbed as I had first suspected was the case. Burglars did not make a promise to return in a set amount of time. Finally, I opened my mouth to speak but, before I could say a word, the door burst open once more and Liza rushed in with a constable trailing not far behind her. The overweight policeman was red faced and out of breath and he took a moment to double over, hands on his knees, and suck in a few breaths before he looked up to us.

"Wh—where are the thugs?" the constable gasped out.

Liza wasn't listening. She saw the state our father was in and ran to him, throwing her arms around him in an embrace when she reached him. He placed his arms around her as well but I saw the sorrow in his eyes as he did and I knew she must feel those arms shaking around her. I cleared my throat and took a step toward the constable.

"They just left," I told him. "But I don't think you're going to catch them."

I allowed my eyes to cast over him, out of shape and out of breath as he was. He bristled.

"I would like to file a report with your station," I said and he nodded, clearing his throat as he glanced about the room to see that nothing was in disarray. He would not have much of a crime scene to investigate.

"I will need statements from anyone present," he told me, eying my father and my sister huddled together behind me. I gave a curt nod of understanding.

"You may question them here and then I will come with you for the official filing."

He narrowed his eyes as me, clearly perturbed by a woman giving him permission to do anything but this was my home and I was feeling rather protective of it at the moment. I remained unfazed as I sidestepped so that he could move beyond me to my petrified family.

"Mr. Porter," the constable said to my father, not a trace of empathy in his official tone. My father released Liza and straightened to look the policeman in the eye. The warmth he held for my youngest sister vanished in an icy glare at the constable. I was taken aback by it. I knew that my father had never placed much trust in the local constabulary but to show such evident hatred, especially now that we had a need for law enforcement, was a surprise to me. The constable continued as though he hadn't detected my father's piercing gaze. "I will need for you to tell me precisely what happened here tonight."

"No need," my father grunted. "I won't be filing a report."

"Papa!" I shouted, running to his side. "What do you mean you won't file a report? Those men came into your shop and assaulted you!"

Liza's eyes grew wide in horror as she gazed up at our father but he only clenched his jaw and turned that penetrating gaze on me.

"We will not be filing a report, Charlotte. That is enough."

Stubborn. He always had been. But I was too. I turned to the constable.

"I would like to file a report. I was assaulted as well. One of them held a knife to my throat."

I heard the small, delicate gasp from my sister and a corresponding grunt from my father.

"Charlotte," my father warned. "You're frightening Liza."

"I'm frightening Liza?" I asked. A horrible laugh escaped me at that. "Father, you were just accosted by two hired thugs and you are concerned that my language might frighten Liza? Why are you being so difficult? Why don't you cooperate with this policeman?"

My father's lip curled in anger in a way that I had never seen before. It forced me back a step.

"Enough, Charlotte," he growled. "Leave it alone."

I stared at him for a moment, stunned by his utter lack of cooperation. He was the victim here. He had done nothing wrong. I knew of his distrust for the police and I knew that he had been acting much unlike himself since the death of my mother but a crime had been committed here. I would not stand idly by and allow such men to get away with such abhorrent behavior. I looked away from my father then and back to the constable.

"I will come with you to the station," I told him, feeling my father's penetrating glare boring into my back as I did so. "And I will tell you what occurred here tonight. Seeing as my father does not seem willing to."

The constable nodded and headed for the door, kindly holding it open for me as he did. I glanced back at my father as I exited. I put all the steely resolve I could into my stare, hoping that the wordless admonishment was enough to convey my disappointment in him. My gaze was met with an angered one of his own and the force of it blew me right out the door and onto the street.

The constable joined me a short time later after bidding a goodbye to my family that was not returned. He cleared his throat, clearly uncomfortable from the witnessing of a familial squabble and urged me on down the road. I followed him the short distance to the police station and went inside with him.

He led me to a small desk in the corner of the room and began to shuffle through some paperwork upon it. I allowed my eyes to wander as he did so and they caught on the sight of a familiar man on the opposite side of the room. He was older, with grey hair and a stomach that protruded over the waistband of his tired old suit. I recognized him immediately from countless newspaper articles I had seen before. The police commissioner. That was odd, I thought. The police commissioner rarely left his offices in the center of London and, when he did, it was never to journey to a town so far away from the city center and so unimportant in the minds of the notable and the elite.

I watched him curiously. He was behind a pane of glass in the only office this police station contained. It was typically given to the local chief but the visit of the police commissioner himself must have commanded it to be surrendered for his use. He was leaning against the desk talking genially with a man who sat in the chair in front of him. The man's back was to me so I could not see his face but I could tell, from his expensive dress and the cordial way he was speaking to the police commissioner, that he was someone of great importance. He leaned back in his chair, clasping his hands behind his head as he did, entangling them with his dark blonde curls.

"Miss Porter," someone spoke and I glanced at the constable staring at me expectedly.

He had set aside a fresh sheet of paper and a pen and was looking up at me once more. He urged me to tell him what had happened and so I did. I left no detail out. I did not see the purpose in concealing anything that had occurred. We were the victims, after all. We had nothing to fear from the law. Strange, then, that my father had felt that we did.

I felt an odd sensation pulling at me, warning me not to tell this constable everything. For some reason, I found myself leaving out the part in which the thugs had told my father he had four days. I could not explain why I did it. Only that I felt that I must. My father's peculiar attitude and the austerity of the threat made it seem out of place in my story of a random attack. It made it seem less random, as though we had been targeted. Suddenly, I realized that we might have been.

My story dropped off upon that realization and I found myself giving the constable only the barest details. He became frustrated with me when I could not give an adequate description of the intruders and led me to the door before too much time had elapsed. I felt compelled to go with him, though my mind was swimming with this new revelation.

My father had exhibited no signs of shock that such an event had occurred. He had not asked the men what they wanted or what they meant by their threat. Because he had understood it, had perhaps even expected it. This had been no random attempt at robbery.

I felt a cold dread settle in the pit of my stomach and knew that I had to get home as swiftly as I could. This matter needed urgent attending to. I thanked the constable perhaps too profusely and then turned on my heel down the road, rejecting his offer to see me home so late at night. I had the strangest sensation that whatever danger awaited me, it was not on these dark streets but rather within my own home.

Something quickened my pace as I set out. I'm not sure what it was. The night air was stifling but quiet. I felt sweat break out on the back of my neck, felt my heart begin to race, felt my feet practically running across the pavement. Then I heard the screams. I saw the smoke and the bright, crackling blaze. There was a loud pop and my father's shop sign fell from its hinges, burning, to the ground below. The words Porter's Books obscured in black soot. I followed the trail of flames from it to the shop ahead. It was ablaze.

My mouth fell open as the glass shattered. I gazed at the people around me. Neighbors, merchants, townsfolk. But not my father and not my sister. They were nowhere in sight.

My eyes darted from the gathered crowd to the burning shop and back again. There was no sign of help. No fire brigade, no constables, nothing. My mind made the connection after my feet had already begun to move. My father and my sister were still in that house, surrounded by flames, choking on smoke. Someone had to save them. But no one was here. I knew what I had to do. Covering my nose and mouth with my sleeve in the crook of my elbow, I ran, quickly but carefully, straight into my family's burning home.

2 A Debt Owed

Inside the fiery shop, the smoke was so thick that it stung my eyes and threatened to blind me. I kept my nose and mouth covered, breathing through the thin fabric of my cheap gown. I glanced from one corner of the room to the other and saw nothing but crumbling shelves, burnt up books, and flame. Above me, the rafters creaked, threatening to snap any moment and bring the second-floor apartment crumbling down on top of the shop and everyone in it. I pulled my sleeve away and choked. "Liza! Papa!"

But the smoke was too heavy and I sputtered a cough. Even if either of them had responded to my cry, I would not have heard it above my own coughing and the cracking of the beams above me. I wiped my eyes and replaced my sleeve over my nose. I moved forward. I had to keep moving forward.

I stumbled through the shop to the door at the back and shoved hard. It fell under my weight, the wood splintering and cracking, borne brittle by the rapidly increasing heat. It was not so hot in the hall beyond. So, the fire must have originated in the shop. I pushed through the smoke, squinting through the haze. I placed a hand on the doorknob to the workshop and hissed, pulling back at the scalding metal. Instead, I lowered my shoulder and pushed. The second door buckled as easily as the first and swung open on its hinges to reveal another room shrouded in smoke.

"Liza!" I cried, desperation clawing at my heart, smoke choking my lungs. I coughed again as I screamed. "Papa!"

"Charlotte?" the voice was quiet, timid, scared. It came from behind the printing press. I shoved books and racks out of my way and ran to it. My father and my sister huddled together behind the large chunk of machinery. They stared up at me, wide eyed and fearful. I helped my father to his feet as Liza rose hesitantly behind him.

"We have to go," I told them, expressing the urgency as best I could. "Now."

"How?" my father asked. "The back door has been blocked and the shop is on fire."

"Not all of it. There's a path straight through the middle. But it won't be open long. We have to go now!"

I pulled them along, back toward the hallway, toward our only exit. They did not seem to want to move. I had to shout at them more than I cared to but if I did not get them out, they would perish here amidst their books. I was forceful with them, shoving and shouting until we reached the shop. Then they came to a dead halt and I could see why. Portions of the ceiling had fallen onto the floor below and a large beam was stretched across most of the floor, shrouded in flame. I covered my mouth and nose with my sleeve and indicated for them to do the same. They did. There was a small opening on the opposite side of the beam, enough for us to slip through, but closing by the second. I pointed to it. Liza looked up at me, wide eyed, and shook her head. I gazed down at her intensely and she understood my meaning. She had to. We had no choice.

Liza went first, boldly sprinting across the floor and leaping through the crack over the beam. I watched her proudly and then turned to my father, nodding for him to go. But he wasn't looking at me. He was staring, wide eyed, at the space that Liza had just been. His hands were shaking. I took them and he finally turned to me. I stared deeply into those familiar eyes. There was not a trace of the anger with which he had looked at me before in them. I gave him a curt nod and a little shove and followed him forward.

We both made it through the crack and onto the other side. Though it required far more pushing and prodding from me than I had hoped. The opening closed the moment we were on the other side of it, a nearby shelf falling, flaming, over to close the gap. We exited the building to join Liza on the street. I withdrew my sleeve from my face and gulped in the stale night air. I would never have previously called London air fresh or exuberant but, at that moment, it was the most delicious thing I had ever tasted.

I heard the people around us gasp and whisper to one another as Liza ran to our father and embraced him. A second later, I heard the sirens and I straightened myself in time to see the fire brigade arrive just as the roof collapsed. I glanced back at my father's shop. It was in ruins. The fire had spread to the upper floors and, undoubtedly, the workshop beyond. Had my father chosen a less flammable occupation, perhaps some of his work could have been saved but, as it happened, the fire brigade was too late to do anything more than contain the fire to our shop and our shop alone and wait for the flames to die down.

I joined my family a few feet away and we all huddled together and watched in agony as the bookshop that had been in our family for generations burnt to the ground and, with it, our livelihood. I saw tears in my father's eyes for the second time in my life that night. The first had been upon the death of my mother only a year ago. And now this.

We remained until the neighbors had all returned to their homes, until the fire brigade had put out the last of the flames and sped away, until the smoke cleared and left behind naught but smoldering rubble. Then I gently guided my family away from the destruction and into a carriage. We rode in silence, all of us wide eyed and tearful, covered in soot and ash. But we were alive. No matter how great our losses had been this day, we were safe. We were alive.

The carriage dropped us off at a familiar shop. I tapped lightly on the door and waited. In a few moments, my brother in law appeared in the threshold, rubbing sleep from his eyes as he gazed in surprise at the three of us. I imagined we were quite the sight. My father would not meet his eyes as he let us in, and we entered the shop and ascended the stairs to the living quarters above. My sister was waiting, arms folded and face scrunched in concern. Liza ran to her the moment we entered and they embraced but Victoria kept her eyes on me.

"The shop is gone," I said in explanation of our presence. My sister and her husband were far too polite to ask directly and, as the intruders, it was our burden to share the news. Victoria's mouth dropped open and her hand flew to cover it. I heard Benjamin, her husband, curse behind me. I continued my explanation, though I imagined they had gathered what had happened from the ash on our clothes and soot staining our skin. "It burned down."

"How?" the question was out of her mouth in an instant. I blinked at her for a moment, realizing for the first time that I did not, in fact, know what had started the fire. I turned toward my father and was surprised to see him already looking at me, that intense glare back in his eyes.

"Charlotte went to the police," he said, as if that were somehow an explanation. I felt my mouth drop open this time.

"What does that have to do with-" I stopped myself as understanding dawned on me. "You think those thugs are behind this?"

"Thugs?" Victoria interrupted, glancing from me to my father and back again.

I hardly heard her. I felt as though pieces of the evening were falling into place and the bigger picture at play was one that I did not care for. The back door had been blocked. My father had told me as much during my attempt at rescuing them from the workshop. It had been blocked he had said. I had assumed, in the moment, that meant it was inaccessible due to falling rubble but that did not make sense upon reflection. I had noticed, myself, that the fire must have originated in the shop. So neither rubble nor flame would have blocked the back door which meant that the only blockage there would have been placed there. Intentionally.

"Are you saying this is my fault?" I asked my father, ignoring my sister for the moment. The fight went out of him then. He sighed and his shoulders slumped. He rubbed his forehead and, when he looked back up at us, his eyes were soft.

"No Charlotte," he said then, shaking his head sadly. "It isn't your fault. It's mine."

"No Papa!" Liza shouted. "It's not your fault. If those thugs are truly responsible then we can tell the police and they-"

"No one is going to the police," he said, firmly but kindly. "Not anymore. You saw what happened when we did."

The room fell silent.

"What happened, William?" Benjamin asked calmly and I found myself silently grateful for his presence.

"I- I made a mistake. I got into debt with some... less than reputable people," My father confessed, scratching his beard with a hand as he did. I had never seen him look so defeated. "Those men who visited our shop this evening were sent to warn me about what would happen if I did not pay back my debts. When Charlotte went to the police... they must have followed her and... burned down the shop to remind us who we are dealing with. These people, they can't be reasoned with. The only thing they respond to is money. The only way out is to pay them back."

We all stared at him.

"Papa," Victoria said slowly. "What do you owe them money for?"

He looked away then, staring at his shoes, a pained expression on his face. I steeled myself for the answer that I knew I would not like.

"I got into gambling again," he admitted and the air was sucked right out of the room. Victoria sighed. Benjamin straightened. Liza gasped. I just watched as a broken man admitted his faults to his family. "After your mother died I couldn't- I didn't- it broke me, girls. It really did. I tried so hard to be strong for you but I... I'm not strong."

Liza sniffled.

"How much?" Victoria asked then. I glanced at my sister, ever the blunt one.

"Four... four thousand," my father spoke and every jaw in the room dropped. Four thousand was far more than his shop would make in a year, most likely more than it would make in five, even with his fancy new upper-class editions. I felt the need to sit and so I slumped onto a nearby chaise.

"Damn, William," Benjamin spoke. He ran a hand through his hair and looked around at all of us. "I suppose you'll be needing a place to stay then. I'll grab some extra quilts."

"Benjamin," Victoria flashed her husband a warning look from the opposite side of the room but she was met with an exhausted sigh.

"They're family, Victoria," he reminded her. "They're staying. For as long as they need."

The last part was directed at us. He met my eyes as he said it. I gave him a small smile of gratitude but pulled it back the moment he left the room. I was suddenly feeling quite ill. It took Benjamin no time at all to get our father settled comfortably in the small guest room that was hardly more than a linen closet. As he did, Victoria doled out blankets and pillows for Liza and I to huddle together in the living room. I knew she was not pleased with the arrangement. Victoria had always been proud and she had taken her marriage as her freedom. When mother had died, she had taken it the hardest. She felt that it was her duty to ensure that we were cared for and she had been saying for quite some time that father had not been doing a very good job at it on his own. She eyed me as I settled in next to a sniffling Liza. Because of our bond, I knew what she intended to communicate. We were family. That, she would acknowledge. But she had a new family to care for and she and Benjamin could not afford to feed us all on the coin of a butcher.

"Liza and I will search for jobs tomorrow," I whispered in the dark. Liza stopped her sniffling and turned to look at us, wiping her eyes with the back of her hand. When she saw me looking up at Victoria and the way that Victoria was looking down at us, as though we were simply two more mouths to feed, she nodded fervently to show her agreement. "First thing. We can help father pay off this debt."

"I don't want danger brought to my house," Victoria warned lowly. I could only nod in understanding. I did not want that either. But I could make no promises. My sister had made a life for herself here. A life of comfort and happiness. As much as she loved us, she loved Benjamin as well and we were threatening the home that they had made together. I gave her another nod to show that I understood precisely what worried her. She straightened her back and left the room, blowing out the candles as she went.

I turned to face Liza as she cuddled up next to me. I felt her breath on my neck as I stroked her hair to soothe her and waited for her breathing to even with sleep. That was when I heard the quiet argument of my sister and her far too patient husband.

***

The next morning, we awoke with grumbling stomachs and the faint memory that we had not eaten dinner the night before. Benjamin had gone out early to get us some newspapers and Liza and I sat perched at the table going over the classifieds as my sister made breakfast. My father joined us but ate very little and spoke even less. He did not care for Liza's and my search for employment but it frankly did not matter. We were without the shop that had been in our family for generations, without our trade, and without our money. We would have to do what had to be done to secure lives for ourselves outside of my sister's house and to pay off my father's debts as soon as possible.

"There is an opening for a seamstress at Madam Delvaux's shop," I told Liza, smiling down at her. "You would be very good at that. You're quite the seamstress."

"Always had the straightest stitches in the family," Victoria smiled down at her as she set her plate in front of her.

"There are quite a few seamstress positions open, Liza. You should apply for them all."

She nodded happily as she tucked into her bread and jam. Victoria caught my eye over her head and I caught the unspoken communication there as well. Liza was young. Perhaps too young. She may not be offered employment no matter how many interviews she went on. I had thought of that. Of course, I had. But we still had to try.

"Father," Liza said suddenly. "There is an opening for an assistant at Abbott's Bookshelf. Perhaps you could find work in the literature industry still."

My father turned to look at his youngest daughter and we all held our breath. He was unhappy, that was for certain, but he nodded through his gritted teeth just the same. I felt myself release a breath in relief. This was, after all, his debt that we were trying to pay off. He should contribute to the cause no matter how severely it wounded his pride to ask for work from a former competitor. I rose from the table then and kissed Liza, then father, on top of their heads.

"I'm off then," I announced. "I'd like to get a jump on my interviews. I have plenty to go on and you know what they say. The early bird gets the-"

"Job," Benjamin finished incorrectly, grinning at his joke. I rolled my eyes and kissed my sister on the cheek before heading for the door.

It was another horribly humid day out and I found myself itching to remove my gloves as I walked, palms sweating against the coarse cloth. I knew it was inappropriate to do so, however, and I needed to look as presentable as possible for my day of job searching. The first shop that I called upon was a small boutique which specialized in woman's hats. I tried my hardest to sell them on the similarities of book binding and hat making but fell woefully short on the latter and they practically hit my behind with the door on my way out.

The next position was for a governess post but the lady of the house seemed dissatisfied with my level of education. Apparently, learning everything myself from the books I bound was not equivalent, in her eyes, to the worldly knowledge she wished her children exposed to. She was polite but hinted strongly that I would not be contacted.

It went on like this for the entire morning and I found myself feeling rather discouraged as I entered the next post on my list. After this, I would retire for lunch. My feet were aching and the dull pangs of hunger were beginning in my stomach. I entered the office of Mr. Patrick Welford near midday and approached his temporary receptionist with a smile. I knew she was merely temporary because I was here to apply for the permanent post. I introduced myself and my reason for stopping by and she smiled sweetly at me.

"If you will take a seat in the lobby, Miss Porter. Mr. Welford has had a very busy morning, but he will be with you as soon as possible," I thanked her and turned to go but she stopped me. "Miss Porter. Perhaps it is not my place to say but, speaking as a fellow working woman, you should know that Mr. Welford does not seem at his best today. He seems rather... distant. I thought it only fair that I warn you."

I nodded my thanks and turned to sit in the lobby. I placed my bag upon my lap and grasped it as I gazed about the room around me. Mr. Welford's office looked the same as any other London lawyer's office I had ever seen. The chairs that I sat upon had certainly seen better days but, even so, the green upholstery indicated wealth. Wood paneling decorated every inch of available wall space. He had beautiful inlaid bookshelves containing a number of prominent legal titles and even a full library of encyclopedias. My eyes scanned them with curiosity to see that he did, in fact, have every letter, but they froze over the volume for the letter Q. Something was different about that book. The spine had been broken but not from the normal act of reading. There were spaces of air on either side of it as if the opposite side of the book, the side in which you would open it, had stretched beyond its capacity and, for some reason, could not be closed.

My attention was drawn away from the strange volume by the sound of the bell at the door tinkling to indicate that someone else had entered. I glanced over to see the most handsome man I had ever seen enter the office. He was dressed like a gentleman in a suit that looked practically new. He removed his hat to reveal a mop of dark blonde curls. He approached the receptionist and smiled. She practically melted at the sight of it. I restrained the urge to roll my eyes. I had met my fair share of men like this. Rather than watch this flirtatious exchange, I reached for a nearby newspaper and began to read.

"Good morning, Miss," the handsome stranger spoke. "I was wondering if Mr. Welford was in. I have some business I need to discuss with him."

"He is in, Sir," she said in a voice much higher than the one she had used with me. I couldn't contain my smirk. "But he's had a very busy morning and I'm afraid that young lady is waiting for him as well. But perhaps if your business is urgent..."

I felt the woman's eyes upon me. I knew she was weighing her options. This man was clearly more important than me and Mr. Welford would most likely be far more interested in his business than mine.

"Not at all," the man replied smoothly. "I'm perfectly suited to waiting my turn. Thank you, Miss...?"

"Calvert," she told him eagerly. "Jane Calvert."

"Well Miss Calvert. It's a pleasure to meet you. Might I ask you a question? You said your boss has had a busy morning. Did you mean he had many clients to attend to?"

I lowered my newspaper a bit and peered over the top. The man was leaning against the desk, giving Miss Calvert his full attention and she seemed utterly captivated by the notion. I watched his cool blue eyes bore into her and she responded with a clear eagerness to please. Surely, she knew that a man of his class could never be interested in a receptionist. I narrowed my eyes. What was he up to?

"No sir," she answered. "Not a client all morning. What I mean is, Mr. Welford came in late and asked me to leave him to his work. I've only seen him once or twice since. He does not look well. I told him he should go home but he claimed he needed to be here."

"Poor Mr. Welford," the stranger clucked his tongue. "It isn't wise to remain in the office when sick."

"I don't think he's ill, sir. But he is... acting odd."

"How peculiar. Did he have any visitors yesterday who could have upset him?"

Miss Calvert glanced about her, chewing on her bottom lip as if indecisive on whether she should tell this stranger her boss' business. She was so caught up in her own speculation that she didn't seem to find it odd that such a stranger should care at all about her employer's previous visitors. In the end, she gazed into those blue eyes and gave it up.

"The police were here."

"Were they?" he asked, interested. He raised a brow at the information. Then he turned and saw me for the first time. I did not look away, as I perhaps should have, but I assumed that averting my gaze would only draw attention to it and that would be some sort of admission of guilt. Though I had not been doing anything I was not supposed to. Perhaps it was considered rude to eavesdrop but the space in this lobby was not infinite and the two of them were in no way speaking in hushed tones. So, when his eyes met mine, I held their gaze. His lips spread into a slow smile and he told Miss Calvert, without looking her way. "I'll have a seat then."

Her shoulders fell at his sudden disinterest and her eyes travelled to me as he walked my way. Her lips puffed into a pout and her eyes turned to a glare when the stranger sat in the chair right next to mine. I only raised my paper back to my eye line and continued to read. But he was too close to be blocked out and I could still see him settling in from my peripheral vision. I waited until Miss Calvert settled back into her own seat before I whispered, from behind the newspaper. "You're rather well dressed for a detective."

He glanced quickly my way in the briefest show of surprise before his eyes slid back to Miss Calvert to ensure she hadn't noticed and landed, finally, on the pocket watch he had withdrawn and now held in his hand.

"You're rather observant for a receptionist," he responded. I snorted softly.

"I'm not a receptionist," I corrected.

"No. But you're hoping to be."

He nodded at the door to Mr. Welford's office beyond and I felt my lips part in surprise. How had he known that? Then I realized that I had been looking at the classifieds and I sighed. He chuckled softly at my side.

"What's he done?" I asked, making my own gesture toward the door.

"Nothing, as far as I know."

"What's he suspected of doing?"

He smiled.

"I would never threaten to tarnish a man's reputation on mere suspicion," he told me, eyes sparkling as they met mine. I cleared my throat and turned the page of my newspaper, though I hadn't truly read any of it in some time. The door to Mr. Welford's office opened just then and the man himself glanced our way and nodded a brief acknowledgement before crossing the floor to his loyal receptionist. I could not help but notice the dark circles under the man's eyes and the way his hair stood on end, as it would of one who had run their hands through it one too many times, as he bent his head to whisper to Miss Calvert.

"If I were going to hide something valuable," I began in a low murmur as I watched the two of them speaking. The stranger's attention was entirely on me now. "I would hide it somewhere that no one would ever look. Say a seldom used encyclopedia."

The man's eyes found the encyclopedias on the opposite side of the room.

"Miss Porter?" Mr. Welford said and I stood as he made his way back to his office, expecting me to follow.

"The letter Q should do the trick, I believe," I finished and then followed after my potential future employer, not daring a glance back at the strange detective.

I entered an office that was much smaller than the lobby beyond and sat in a chair that was much more worn. Mr. Welford crossed to stand behind his desk and stared down at the references I had brought with me. They were not impressive. They contained my father, my brother in law, and a woman whom I had done some sewing for on the side one summer. He grunted when he finished and tossed the paper on top of the untidy pile on his desk.

"You are here to apply for the position of receptionist."

It was not a question but I answered anyway. "Yes, sir."

"You have no experience as a receptionist."

"I do not. But I worked in my father's book shop my whole life. I have experience in keeping ledgers as well as making appointments. And my experience in book binding-"

"Allow me to stop you there, Miss Porter," he said. His pinched the bridge of his nose with his forefinger and thumb and made a sound entirely of exhaustion. I wondered when he had last slept and what it was that kept him awake. "This is a legal office. My permanent receptionist would have to have some legal knowledge."

"My father's shop has bound quite a few legal volumes. I often read the books as we bind them. I believe I may have some beginners insight on case law as well as-"

"You read about it?" he asked, quirking his brow. "That's all? You have no formal education. No real references. No work experience outside of your father's shop."

He sighed. I opened my mouth but then decided that my forthcoming assertion that a formal legal education was hardly more than reading books as well would not be a welcome one with such an educated man. An educated man foolish enough to hide his secrets in an office encyclopedia. Or so I had presumed.

"I'm sorry, Miss Porter. But I don't think you quite match the qualifications that I am looking for."

I took a breath. I had been expecting this decision but it did nothing to soften the blow. Knowing that I was about to make my way home for lunch with nothing to show for my morning's efforts, I stood to thank Mr. Welford but, before I could, the door to his office burst open. In the threshold stood a fully uniformed constable.

"Mr. Patrick Welford," the man said, all manner of authority in his tone. A few more constables entered the room alongside him.

"What is the meaning of this?" Mr. Welford demanded.

"You're under arrest."

He gaped at them.

"Under arrest?" he asked, appalled. "For what?"

They did not answer as they moved forward with handcuffs.

"This is outrageous! Do you know who I am? Do you know who I represent? Have you heard of my father?"

Mr. Welford carried on as the constables led him out of the office, through the lobby, and into the street beyond. I followed them, drawn by the strange scene and somehow unable to keep my feet from moving. Miss Calvert followed as well but approached the constable herself, demanding answers as to why her boss was being arrested. I stood on the steps of the office, watching the scene before me. Mr. Welford continued his pleas as they led him away and, when they no longer worked, began shouting at Miss Calvert to contact his brother. She paled and scurried away to do as he bid that instant.

"Q, huh?" a familiar voice spoke and I spun around to see the strange detective from the lobby leaning against the threshold. He held up a hand and a beautiful, ornate, golden pocket watch dangled from its chain wrapped around his finger. "How did you know?"

"That's what was in there?" I asked, mesmerized by the glinting object. He smiled and handed the watch to a nearby constable who took it off with him as he headed after the rest of the policemen back to the station.

"How did you know it was in the book?"

"I've seen enough hollowed out books in my day to know the look of them," I told him, crossing my arms as I did. "No honest man would ever carve away the written word unless he is hiding something he shouldn't."

He smiled at that. I felt my stomach begin to grumble and knew I should be on my way home.

He stepped forward and extended a hand. "Alexander Langley,"

"Charlotte Porter," I answered, shaking his hand.

He looked me over as though I were some strange curiosity.

"I suppose I won't be getting that position," I said, glancing back at the legal office behind him. "So, if you'll excuse me, I must be returning home. I'm certain my sisters are worried sick."

"I think it's safe to say that Mr. Welford will not be needing a receptionist for quite some time," he said with that crooked grin of his but it was the words that he spoke next which froze me in place. "So why don't you come work for me?"

3 An Offering

"Work for you," I repeated slowly, feeling the words on my tongue as if they'd settled there, utterly dumbstruck by the suggestion. I watched his lips curl into a charming smile and had to confess that I might have understood Miss Calvert's abject fascination with him more than I cared to admit. He was, indeed, quite handsome. Even I, a lowly born merchant class girl, must admit that. Though he had the air about him of one who knew of his own attraction and I had been drawn in and destroyed by such an attitude before.

"Is that so absurd?" he asked innocently. Then he sighed, having correctly understood my expression to mean that I did, in fact, find it quite absurd. So he offered an explanation. "I have been in need of a partner for some time now. Your capacity for observation is astounding. You noticed, from across the room, that book on the shelf was hollowed out."

"I am somewhat of a book expert, having worked with them my whole life," I explained, waving off my observation as a mere trick of my trade. But he was not so easily swayed.

"You made the connection that he must have hidden something of importance there."

"Why else hollow out a book?"

"You surmised who I was and what I was after mere moments after meeting me."

"You were not subtle."

He smiled at that. "I rather thought I was."

"Then your clandestine efforts need work."

"You are an intelligent woman," He praised and I felt my cheeks heating at his words. No man in all my life had ever spoken such a sentence to me and, though my brain was warning me against falling for the flattery, my ego could not help but soar at it. "You are perceptive to the extreme, whether or not you choose to acknowledge it, and you have one other quality that I would value highly in a potential partner."

Curiosity getting the best of me, I asked. "What is it?"

"When you suspected that man may be hiding something and that I was there to figure it out, you effortlessly chose the side of good. You chose to disclose what you thought you knew to the authorities."

I stared at him. He was right. I hadn't thought of it that way at the time, of course, but I had decided to tell him what I suspected. In truth, I hadn't even considered keeping the information to myself. It had been clear that something was going on with Mr. Welford and that this gentleman was here to discover what that was. So, I had wasted no time in assisting the man whom I had presumed, correctly, was on the side of the law. He was watching me now, a look of amused curiosity plain in his expression. I regarded him with suspicion and, admittedly, with an abundance of curiosity of my own. After a moment, he held an arm out to me.

"Come with me to my office," he offered. "We can discuss the terms of your employment there."

I stared out at the offered arm. He had been correct to presume that I was a law-abiding citizen. He seemed to believe that I possessed some sort of perceptive quality and investigative capability. I eyed him carefully. He was well dressed and spoke as an educated man would. He had just assisted the police in an investigation of theft. I had witnessed it. He did not seem the sort of man to fear. Though I had recently had far too many run ins with that sort. Remembering the thugs that had threatened my father and burned down his shop brought fresh clarity to the situation. This man was offering employment. I had been out all morning seeking such an opportunity. No matter my reservations, it occurred to me that I was not in a position to turn down any job offer. No matter what it was or how unseemly it may be for a woman to practice in such a field.

So I took his arm, slipping my own through the crook in it, and he led me, smiling, to the curb where a carriage, vastly lovelier than the rented one which had brought me into town, was waiting. He opened the door and I climbed inside, seating myself on one side while he sat on the opposite. Once he had settled in, he knocked on the top of the box and the driver hurtled off down the busy London streets. I gripped the seat beneath me for a moment before making a conscious effort to relax and folding my white knuckles in my lap as I sat back against the seat. I noticed that he was watching my every movement carefully but making none of his own as if he were afraid that any abrupt undertaking might alarm me and I would dive from the coach like a startled housecat.

"I've never met a detective with his own carriage and driver," I told him in an effort to begin a conversation and evade this quiet awkwardness. He smirked.

"I'm not a detective," he confessed. My surprise and following discomfort must have been evident because he hurried on with his explanation. "I am a consulting investigator. The police come to me with their more... elusive cases and I offer my services for a fee."

"So that is what you were doing at Mr. Welford's office? Investigating?"

"I was. In fact, I had come to the end of my investigation. I felt rather certain that Patrick Welford had the item in his possession."

"The pocket watch."

"Yes. The pocket watch. It was a family heirloom. His father had given it to his younger brother rather than him. Jealousy and the need for money drove him to steal it."

"Need for money? Mr. Welford was a practicing attorney."

"A practicing attorney with a dying clientele and massive gambling debts."

I sat back in my seat. The mention of gambling debts made my knees feel wobbly. It was an unwelcome reminder of my own family's precarious position and the very reason that I was seated in this carriage with this strange man presently. I felt that I needed to force the continuance of the conversation to distract myself from the wave of nausea now threatening to drown me.

"His own brother had him arrested?" I questioned. "He is pressing charges?"

"Not all brothers are close," He answered me with a sad smile.

I looked down at my hands in amazement. I could not imagine ever pressing charges against Liza or Victoria no matter what they did. We were family. We were sisters. They could not possibly do anything to me that would make me stop loving them or that would make me wish to see them in chains. But Mr. Welford's brother disagreed with me. For a pocket watch, a simple object, he would have his brother cast in chains. I knew that not all siblings were close but, in my lower-class world, family was all one had. We did not have expensive possessions or incredible riches. All we had was the love of one another and the distribution of the work evenly amongst us. I knew that Liza and Victoria would not see me in chains either though Liza's was more out of love and Victoria's more out of the realization that my imprisonment would mean more responsibility and work for her to bear.

I did not realize how long I had been silent until the carriage came to a stop and Mr. Langley stepped out and held out a hand to help me down. I took it and lowered myself gently to the ground below. I looked up to see the most charming manor I had ever seen. I had never found myself in this part of London before. Of course, I had never had reason to journey this far into the wealthier parts of town but every house in Mr. Langley's quiet, secluded neighborhood was exquisite and the one in front of us was perhaps the grandest of them all. For not the first time, I found myself wondering just how much I had yet to uncover about this gentleman investigator. He called out a thanks to the driver and then walked me to the door. It opened before we reached it and a butler stood just inside, smiling and offering a hand for our coats and hats. We handed them to him and he nodded back in welcome, thin lines of his mouth spreading into a smile at the sight of me.

"Welcome home, Sir," He said with the professional warmth of one who quite enjoys his job.

"Thank you, Bernard. This is-"

But his introduction was interrupted by the appearance of a beautiful young woman in an elaborate lavender gown. She was nearly my own age though perhaps a year or two younger. She had an elegant figure and striking blue eyes which darted to and fro as she passed through the hall, pausing briefly upon a servant dusting a painting on the wall in interest. Her blonde curls cascaded down her shoulders in a beautiful waterfall of molten gold and she twirled a strand around her elegant finger as she marched herself into the room.

"There you are Alexander. I have been wondering where you had gotten to. I didn't even see you leave this morning and I-"

She stopped cold at the sight of me, her inquisitive blue eyes darting from me to the man at my side and back again. I judged who she was by the casual manner in which she addressed my companion and by the ease at which she seemed to conduct herself in the house which she must call home.

"Who-" she began but I interjected.

"Charlotte Porter," I introduced myself kindly. "It's very nice to meet you Mrs. Langley. You have a lovely home."

Her expression changed from blank to amused.

"Oh no," Mr. Langley said, clearing his throat. "Elena is not my wife. She is my sister."

"Oh," I felt my own cheeks reddening as I understood the assumption I had made. "My sincerest apologies."

"It's quite alright," Miss Langley said, waving her hands to clear the awkward air. I was grateful for her grace. She pulled me to the side and grasped my arm as she smiled kindly at me. "It isn't every day that my brother brings a beautiful young woman to our home. You must be quite intriguing."

Mr. Langley cleared his throat again.

"Elena," he said in an attempt at a warning but his voice was too soft. I could tell that he found himself quite unable to admonish her. He continued. "Miss Porter is a candidate for the position of Investigative Partner and Business Assistant."

"Business Assistant?" I asked, turning back to face Mr. Langley at the additional title. He smiled.

"If we should ever part ways, Miss Porter, I would not leave you without a marketable skill. It is impossible for a woman to find employment within the field of investigation but receptionist posts are nearly overwhelming. I conduct quite a bit of business myself. Should you assist me in such matters, it will give you the experience required to apply for even the most advanced reception positions."

I felt my mouth drop open a bit in surprise at his understanding generosity.

"Well, if it's business that drives you, you'll be pleased to know that Mr. Harrison is awaiting your return in your office," Miss Langley said then and her beautiful smile was replaced by a frown. "Do attend to him as quickly as you can. He has been quite insufferable all morning."

Mr. Langley smiled at that and, with a final wink in my direction, Miss Langley was off down another hall to the side. I followed Mr. Langley further into the house and into his office at the end of the entrance hall on the right. Sure enough, another young man was waiting inside. He sat perched on the edge of a large mahogany desk, holding his hat in one hand. He was quite handsome as well but in an entirely different way, with dark brown eyes and matching hair. His face was chiseled into a set of dazzling features and I could see the indication of a lean, muscular frame despite his layers of gentlemanly attire. His eyebrows quirked at our entrance and he broke into a lazy grin at the sight of me.

"Well, well, Alexander," he said as we entered and Mr. Langley shut the door behind us. "I would have been quite content to wait a bit longer had I known you were in the company of such an angel."

He stood from his position on the desk and crossed the room to me. I extended a hand to shake his but he placed a tender kiss upon mine instead. I gazed at him in surprise as Mr. Langley crossed to his desk behind him.

"This one is too smart for your tricks, I'm afraid, Nathaniel," Mr. Langley spoke and Mr. Harrison smiled up at me beneath thick lashes.

"She must be quite special indeed to earn an invitation into your home," Mr. Harrison responded, placing emphasis on the word your that I did not quite understand.

"I think so," Mr. Langley said and I saw him smiling at me from behind Mr. Harrison. I felt my cheeks flush again and scolded myself for the reaction. "I am hoping to make her my new partner. That is, if I can convince her."

Mr. Harrison turned back to Mr. Langley, an amused grin on his face.

"Am I being replaced?" he asked lazily and Mr. Langley smiled.

"Not yet," Mr. Langley teased. "No. Miss Porter is to be my investigative partner. Mr. Harrison is my business partner, you see Miss Porter. But she will be assisting us on matters of business as well."

Mr. Harrison nodded brightly.

"Well, then, she should hear the news I've come to tell you as well," he said, rapping his knuckles on the desk.

"I'm afraid it will have to wait, Nathaniel," Mr. Langley said and then he raised an eyebrow in my direction. "We are in the middle of an interview."

Mr. Harrison looked from Mr. Langley to me and back again. He seemed surprised at the importance that Mr. Langley placed upon my hiring. I felt uncomfortable at my place near the door. I felt my feet shuffling of their own accord in the silence that followed. Then Mr. Harrison simply cleared his throat and smiled.

"Well then, I'll leave you to it," he said, grabbing his hat and coat and heading for the door. "Do stop by soon though, Alexander. As much as you adore your investigations, your father's business cannot wait forever."

With that, he was beyond the doors of the office and I found myself alone with my intriguing potential employer. I raised a brow as I sat in the seat opposite him to which he had gestured the moment his partner had left the room.

"Father's business?" I inquired. He smiled.

"I told you that you were observant," he answered. "Yes. My mother and father live in their country home outside of the city. Elena and I live here for most of the year and take care of the business as well as the social obligations."

I tried hard not to focus on the choice of the word obligation. Did my future employer not care greatly for the London social scene? It seemed to me that it would care very dearly for him, being the eligible, wealthy, handsome young bachelor he was. Also at odds with my knowledge of London upper class society was the fact that he and his sister lived apart from their parents. It was common, for the children of the London elite, to remain abiding in their parent's home until they are married. Though uncommon, I had heard of men leaving home as bachelors to attend to business but never just in the city itself, usually because they were required internationally. Miss Langley, however, I could not explain. For a young woman to choose to live with her older brother rather than her mother was quite odd indeed. The rich young women who sometimes came into the shop with their mothers always seemed to be practically attached to their hips. Most young women found their mate through their mother's social connections. That would be a difficult feat to accomplish if the mother and daughter lived separately.

"What business?" I asked, noticing that Mr. Langley had not taken his eyes off of me as I allowed my thoughts to wander and realizing that he was waiting for a response.

"Investments," He answered as though that word were not as broadly undefined as he left it. I watched him for a moment, wondering just how forward and outspoken I could be around this man. In most circles, it was considered uncouth for a woman to attempt to talk business with a man, especially two unwed people such as ourselves. But the sort of employment that he was proposing indicated that such conversation would be necessary so I dared the question.

"Investments?" I asked and he smiled in what appeared to be approval.

"That curiosity will serve you will in this role."

"The role that I have not accepted yet," I reminded him. Perhaps that was too bold. I would accept the position, of course, because I had to. But, if this were truly the employment negotiation that he claimed it was, he did not need to know how desperate I was. I knew, better than my father, not to show my hand.

"Yet," he answered and even dared a wink. I could not contain my smile as he leaned back in his chair, becoming more comfortable around me now that I had opened the door to this sort of banter. "I cannot give you a precise answer because there isn't one. My father and I use our family's wealth to invest in products and industries that we believe in. And we have made quite a bit of money doing so. I've just returned to London, in truth. I was in America for the past three years on a trip of investment opportunity."

"America?" I asked, stunned.

"Yes. In truth, that is where I discovered my love for investigation. The Americans are not so proprietary as we English. They lack a lot of the restrictive value systems that we employ. So when I, an English gentleman, offered to assist the Pinkerton detectives in their hunt for a Wild West outlaw in the California desert, they did not bat an eye but rather took all the help they could get."

I stared at him in disbelief. The man sitting before me was the very picture of London sophistication and wealth. To envision him in a Wild West setting, chasing after dangerous outlaws, was a bit beyond even my capable imagination. He smiled at my apparent surprise.

"I suppose I developed a bit of a taste for it. So when I returned to London, I went straight to Scotland Yard to offer my services. Which they have already employed multiple times since."

"And that is why you need a partner," I clarified. He nodded.

"Their demands have been increasing and I do have my father's business to attend to as well. Two heads are better than one, as they say. I do believe you and I could solve these cases at a much quicker pace."

I nodded, considering. It did sound like fascinating work and I was unlikely to receive anything so invigorating with the receptionist jobs that I had been applying for. It seemed to be a once in a lifetime opportunity, a wonderful opportunity, perhaps too wonderful. My caution on the matter stayed my hand. If I could be certain of this man's claims, I would accept his invitation in a heartbeat. But you never could be quite certain of anyone's claims. It was rather odd for a gentleman of such wealth to offer me such a job but, then again, everything about Mr. Langley and the lifestyle he chose to live seemed odd and yet captivatingly innovative all the same. I would, perhaps, never know all that I sought to about this man but, judging from his character and the people he surrounded himself with, I thought that perhaps it wasn't the risk that I feared it might be. And I did need the money at any rate.

"I could offer you this amount in the beginning," he told me, pulling a piece of paper and a pen from his desk and jotting down a number. He slid it quietly to my side and I leaned forward to read it. I fought to maintain composure as my eyes roved over the amount. It was nearly double what I could hope to make at even the most respected receptionist position in the city.

"That is very generous," I told him, keeping my eyes firmly on the paper lest they betray my surprise and cause him to reconsider.

"Would you like a trial?" he asked.

"Pardon?" I queried, looking up at him at the question.

"A week," he said, standing from his seat. "A week of working for me and then you can make your decision on whether or not you care to continue. No hard feelings."

I stood hesitantly from my own chair, trying to appear unaffected by the job offer, attempting to remain calm though my heart was flipping at the prospect of employment, at the knowledge that I could help my family.

"A week then," I agreed. He grinned, dimpled cheeks taunting me at the corners of his mouth.

"Wonderful. I will see you here first thing in the morning, Miss Porter."

Then Mr. Langley called for Bernard who appeared in an instant with a pleasant smile and my coat and hat. I collected them from him and allowed him to walk me to the door. Mr. Langley did not follow, electing instead to remain behind in his office and undoubtedly get started on whatever work he had planned to do today. At the door, Bernard opened it and I began to step out but, before I could, someone spoke.

"I knew you'd take the job."

I turned to see Miss Langley. She was sitting on a sofa in the open drawing room, smiling in my direction. She held a bit of needlework in her lap as she sat, straight backed in the way she had been raised to do. Her eyes twinkled mischievously as she gazed out at me. I could not help but return the smile to her.

"It will be nice having another woman around the house. I am looking forward to seeing more of you, Miss Porter. I do hope we can be friends."

With that, I was out on the sidewalk, the door closing behind me. I gazed up at the morning sun, the rumbling returning to my stomach, and remembered the hunger that had pained me only hours before. What a strange morning indeed.

4 Stolen

I had initially decided to walk home as the air felt less heavy than it had before but even the light exercise of walking had me breaking out into a sweat before long due to the uncommon city heat. So I decided to hail a hired cab instead. I paid the man what little coins I had left in my purse and settled in for the jostling ride back to my temporary home. The hansom took me directly to my sister's door and I thanked the gentleman and paid him before stepping onto the sidewalk, hoping that my sister had some leftovers from whatever they had eaten for lunch given the fact that such a meal had long since ended. I hoped that they had not been waiting on me or worried about me in any way. I had been gone much longer than I had anticipated or than I had told them to expect.

I was not aware that something, other than my own tardiness, was amiss until I came to rest just outside the door to the residences above my brother in law's butcher shop. That was when I heard the raised voices from within. I turned the knob and opened the door to find my father sitting in a chair, swaying half drunk. Liza was gripping his right arm to keep him seated and Victoria was bent over in his face, shaking her finger at him in admonishment. Benjamin was the only one who saw me enter. He glanced my way and gave me the smallest shake of the head when our eyes met.

"I cannot believe you would go back there!" my eldest sister was shouting. Her face was red and she paced in front of our father like a mad woman. "To risk your family's lives like that! They've already burned down your shop, Papa. What if they were to come here? To my home? And to make Benjamin come and get you! They know him now! They've seen his face!"

I glanced back to Benjamin and he nodded. So my father had returned to the gambling dens this morning and, if I was understanding my sister's tirade correctly, her husband had been forced to drag him out. I exchanged a glance with Liza. The concern was plain in her eyes. She looked from Victoria's tantrum to me, pleading with me to get involved. I was not sure yet if I should. Benjamin seemed to be warning me against it. He knew, better than anyone, how intense my sister's rage could be. But I knew as well, having grown up with her my entire life, and I knew that, if anyone in this family could face it, it was me.

Though I wasn't certain that I entirely disagreed with her. Our father deserved a bit of admonishment, if I was being honest with myself. He had endangered his family, had endangered Victoria's home and her husband. That was an offense that no woman could abide by. Still, he was her father. As drunk and disorderly as he was.

"I cannot allow you to remain in my home if you endanger my family," Victoria said then, the words falling into the tense air around us. Her anger had subsided somewhat, replaced by what appeared to be simple exhaustion. Now would be the most appropriate time to involve myself in the situation. If any time were appropriate at all. I stepped forward then and the movement drew all eyes to me.

"Perhaps Liza could remain here during the day," I suggested, a measured air of calm in my voice. I needed to diffuse the situation, not restart an argument. "Rather than finding employment. She could watch over father."

"Keep me prisoner here, you mean," my father snapped. I turned my eyes on him and glared. He was not helping his case. Could he not see what he was doing to Victoria? Could he not see the choice that he was forcing her to face? Victoria loved all of us dearly. I knew she did even though her overall gruff manner restricted her from showing us such affection. She would not relish having to decide between her sisters and her husband and the least we could do would be to behave under her roof so that she would not have to make such an atrocious choice. I knew the struggle that my father currently faced well enough but that gave him no excuse to act horrendously at the charity given to him by his eldest daughter.

"If that's what it takes to curb your addiction, then yes," I answered him and I could see the surprise on his face at my choice of words. He was so used to being coddled, so used to our admiration and mother's love but mother was gone and, as I could see it, his actions had forfeited my admiration for the moment. I could help him through this, we all could, but he needed to see that even a daughter's patience had it's limits. I approached him and softly laid a hand on his shoulder. "You are sick, Papa. Allow us to help you through it."

I could tell that he did not appreciate my pointing out his weaknesses in front of the family but he had drawn them into focus himself when he had gone to the gambling hall this morning.

"Very well," He relented, sensing defeat when we all three bore down on him. With a heavy sigh, he stood. "I'm going to lie down. Wake me for dinner."

Then he was gone, disappeared into the guest room without another word.

"I won't be able to work if I stay home with him," Liza said then and my attention turned to her. She seemed rather perturbed by the idea.

"That is probably for the best," Victoria told her. "You're young. Entering the work force at such a young age does not do well for a woman's marketability."

Victoria moved to the kitchen then and began making a sandwich which she must have done once she heard my rumbling stomach. I took my seat at the table and Liza and Benjamin joined us.

"But we need the money," Liza reminded us. "To repay father's debts."

Victoria looked up at that, catching my eye, and I sensed my opportunity.

"I found employment today," I said as she placed the sandwich in front of me. She raised a brow in surprise but remained silent so that I could continue. "I met a very kind young gentleman in need of a... business assistant."

I decided it best not to disclose the full nature of my employment under Mr. Alexander Langley. Victoria would undoubtedly disapprove and we could not afford for me to turn down such an opportunity. Liza sat up a little straighter at my disclosure.

"An assistant?" she inquired. "Like a receptionist?"

I smiled at her. "Precisely the same."

"Then why call it an assistant?" Victoria asked. I looked up at her. There was suspicion in her eyes. I shrugged her question off.

"That was the word he used."

The room fell quiet for a moment and, when I glanced up from my sandwich, both of my sisters were watching me.

"You're certain that this man hired you in a business capacity only?" Victoria asked.

"What are you implying?" I bristled. She sighed.

"That the members of my family have not made the wisest of decisions for themselves as of late. I'm only being cautious. As you should too, Charlotte. This does not sound like it was one of your planned interviews. How did you meet this man?"

"In the waiting room of Mr. Welford, the attorney's, office. He claimed he needed an assistant and noticed that I was looking for work. We went to his office to discuss terms. I met his sister and his business partner, both very affable people. He has hired me on a weeklong trial basis. If he decides that I am unfit, I will be back to searching for a job in a week's time," I answered. I tried to sound casual, unaffected. I tried to shrug off my sister's suspicions but felt her eyes boring into me all the same. Victoria had always had our mother's knack for discerning when one of us was lying to her. Growing tired of the game, I sat down my sandwich and sighed, looking up to meet her eyes at last. "It is a legitimate position, Victoria."

My sister nodded at that and, satisfied, left with Benjamin to return to the business of their shop below. I had told most of the truth, though I had admittedly left out a few details. Not that it mattered. It was none of her affair. I was employed and would be bringing home money that could go to paying my father's debts. That was all that either of my sisters needed to know at the moment.

"She's been that way all morning," Liza said, gathering my plate and heading for the sink to wash it. "On edge. Upset. Ever since we discovered father gone and Ben went to locate him. She has been nearly unhinged."

"She is concerned for her family," I told Liza with a sigh.

"We are her family."

"Not anymore. Not like Benjamin."

"She was talking about you," Liza told me, more quietly, as she scrubbed the plate. "While you were gone. About how you should be out looking for a husband."

I sighed. I was not surprised. Victoria had made it her mission to remind me at every turn that I was still single at twenty five and that I was far past my prime at this point and would be lucky to interest any man at all. Perhaps she was right. Perhaps I was too old now, doomed to live my life alone. But my father needed me now. Someone had to pay off these debts and, if my sisters intended to marry themselves off and remove themselves from our family, then that burden would fall to me and I would bear it gladly.

"I was engaged, remember?" I said to Liza and she looked up at me then. She must have been surprised to hear me speak of my former fiancée. It was a topic that I usually avoided. I smiled encouragingly as I added. "I didn't care for it."

She snorted a laugh but then her face fell serious as she gazed back up at me. "Not every man is as horrendous as Johnathon Birmingham."

"I know," I told her. "But he soured the whole experience for me."

I took her by the shoulders then and turned her to face me. I tucked a strand of the beautiful auburn hair she shared with our older sister behind her ear and smiled down at her.

"I know that Victoria is of the impression that you must wait to marry until I am settled," I said. Liza looked away from me then, a flush creeping up her neck. So this was what she had feared as well. "That isn't the case. You are free to marry whomever and whenever you choose, regardless of my circumstance. Only the rich must wait for their elder sisters to wed. We poor may be lacking in resources but we have a bit more freedom to our lives. You will never have to wait on me. Not that you even could. With that gorgeous face of yours, I imagine men will be knocking down the door the moment we declare you eligible."

Liza beamed at me when I finished and I smiled in return. I truly meant what I had said. Liza was a beautiful girl. She shared the same fair complexion, auburn hair and bright green eyes as Victoria. I shared their eyes but my hair was dark, much more drab, and my complexion was not as fair either. I had retained much more of my father's features while they had favored our mother. I had, however, inherited my mother's most endearing quality. Her fortitude. And I was determined, it seemed, to put that trait to the test.

I assisted Liza with housework for the rest of the afternoon, hoping that a dedicated sweep of the house would result in a much more pleasant Victoria when she joined us for dinner and it mostly worked. The events of the morning had passed, it seemed, from my sister's mind and she was much more keen to talk about the wonderful sale that she and Benjamin had made to a wealthy gentleman who had wandered into the shop. Most of the detail of the story was lost on me as it contained phrases and measurements of a butcher which was a life that I had never lived but I nodded politely along and smiled at her excitement. Our father did not join us for dinner, electing to remain in his rooms instead. I saw Liza looking to his door from time to time and pressed my hand upon hers under the table to communicate that he was fine and more than capable of caring for himself. I imagined, anyway, that he chose to remain in solitude more out of embarrassment than anything else. His intoxication had undoubtedly worn off by now and left him with nothing but the mortifying memory of the events that had unfolded this afternoon.

I found myself feeling rather exhausted at the culmination of dinner and so I excused myself for the evening and fell asleep on my makeshift bed in the living room while the others drank their tea and spoke of the events of the next day.

In the morning, I awoke early due in part to my falling asleep early and in part because of the discomfort of my own sleeping arrangements and the restless sleep they had caused. I readied myself for the day, choosing the nicest gown that I had available to me which was only a dark green day dress borrowed from my eldest sister which was overly tight in the hips and loose at the waist. I readied my hair in a tidy updo and then took a cab to Mr. Langley's home. I expected to have some down time in which I would wait for Mr. Langley to ready himself to leave as the hour was so early but I was surprised to find his carriage already waiting outside of his door as mine pulled up. No sooner had my foot hit the sidewalk beneath the carriage than Mr. Langley was exiting his house, donning his hat, and heading straight for me, a smile alight upon his handsome features.

"Good morning, Miss Porter," he said kindly as he approached. He handed a few coins to the cab driver who had dropped me off and the man took off before I could argue about the payment. Then he held out his arm and I took it. He walked me to the awaiting carriage and helped me inside before climbing in after me and shouting an address to his driver. I vaguely recognized it but had no time to consider what it was before he was speaking again. "My apologies for the abrupt departure, Miss Porter, but we've been given a new case and I think you will find that I do not like to delay."

"Oh," I said, stunned. "I could have arrived earlier if-"

"No, no," He waved his hand dismissively. "You arrived quite early. Earlier than I was expecting, truly. We will arrive in plenty of time."

"Arrive where?"

"Ah yes," He leaned back in his seat, settling in for the ride and for whatever he was about to disclose about our new case. "The London Museum of Art is our destination this morning. They have had a break in and a theft. It appears a painting has been stolen. So I would like to arrive as early as possible and speak to the curator before the museum is open to the public and we must fight a crowd."

I nodded in understanding.

"This is not the first painting to be stolen in the area. In fact, there has been a recent string of stolen paintings. Some of them have been stolen from private residences. Then there is the one from the museum and one from a library as well. The strange thing is that there has been no indication of resale. Typically, a thief steals a piece of art in order to turn around and sell it again for the money. But there has been not even a whisper of these paintings on the market."

Suddenly, our carriage came to a stop and Mr. Langley was exiting. The museum district was not far at all from the wealthy district seeing as that was the class such cultured places usually catered to. He held a hand out and I took it, allowing him to help me onto the sidewalk beyond. I gazed up at the beautiful building ahead of us. The London Museum of Art. I had never been myself but I had heard great things from a neighbor who had been lucky enough to visit the museum in her youth and I had always hoped to visit someday myself. Though this was not a trip of enjoyment, I reminded myself. There was work to be done.

I followed Mr. Langley up to the doors of the massive building and waited as he explained to the guard at the door that we were here on behalf of the police. After a moment of further questioning of our credentials, we were admitted and we found ourselves standing in a large dome, light filtering down upon us from the skylight above. I gazed at all of the beautiful artwork surrounding me just in the foyer. There were sculptures and paintings and murals on the curved walls. It was all so beautiful that I had not even noticed the old curator approaching us.

"Are you the investigator?" the old man spoke and I turned to look at him. I noticed, out of the corner of my eye, that Mr. Langley had been watching me and my face flushed at how absurd I must have looked staring up at the domed ceiling. "Detective Ryland told me I could be expecting a private investigator. Is that you?"

"It is, Sir," Mr. Langley responded, looking at the old man for the first time. "Alexander Langley. Would you mind showing us where the painting was taken from?"

The old man grunted a response and gestured for us to follow and so we did. He led us through multiple hallways, each one of which contained even more beautiful artwork than the last and I tried in vain to keep my eyes off of them and on the hunched back of the elderly curator in front of us. Finally, he rounded a corner and I could see that the police had already roped this section of the museum off for their investigation. He pulled up the rope and we bent to slide in underneath before he replaced it and led us over to an empty glass casing or, at least, what used to be a glass casing. The glass had been shattered and lay in pieces on the floor around the box.

Mr. Langley approached it at once and bent down for a closer inspection. I cocked my head to the side to see around his frame to the empty casing. There did not seem to be anything particularly interesting about this shattered glass. What had happened here seemed clear enough.

"Have you ever had any other break ins before this one?" Mr. Langley asked of the curator though he did not look up at him but rather kept his gaze fixated on the empty casing and the pattern of broken glass at his feet.

"Once," the curator answered. "A week ago, in fact. But nothing was stolen."

Mr. Langley nodded. "I am assuming a museum of this caliber employs a night watchman."

The curator frowned at that. "We do."

"Where is he?"

"Home, I imagine. We fired him after the break in."

"Which break in?"

"This one."

"So he was here for this one and for the first one."

"Yes."

Losing interest in their conversation and finding it difficult to see the purpose in many of Mr. Langley's questions, I began to wander about the room, taking in the artwork around us. I recognized some of the more famous ones from the art history books that I had bound for wealthier clients and university students at my father's shop. A few of the ones in this very room, in fact, had been printed within the very book that I had been binding just days before when those thugs had distracted me from my work and later set it ablaze.

"Did this painting belong to the museum?" Mr. Langley asked behind me.

"No, Sir," the curator answered. "It was on loan from a private citizen. We have not notified him yet. He will not be pleased, I imagine. He has another from the same artist in his home. It is one of his most prized possessions."

"Who is the artist?"

"Vincent Guillard. A modern talent. He's quite young but already his paintings have turned the English art world on its head. He already has quite a few loyal fans who purchase his paintings religiously."

"Is this the only painting that was stolen?" I heard the words come from my mouth before I realized I was speaking them. The curator and Mr. Langley halted their conversation and glanced up at me.

"Who are you?" the curator asked then as if he noticed me for the first time.

"This is Miss Porter," Mr. Langley introduced. "She is my partner."

"Your partner?" The curator looked between us with a raised brow. "But she's a... a woman."

"I'm quite aware," Mr. Langley answered easily. "As is she, I imagine."

I bit back my smile.

"Now, would you care to answer her question?" Mr. Langley prodded. "Was this the only painting that was stolen?"

"Of course," the curator bristled. "I would have told you if it wasn't."

But Mr. Langley's attention was no longer on the old curator. He was watching me. I could feel his eyes on me even though my back was to him. I was admiring a rare Monet which was displayed just next to the broken glass and missing painting. I could practically feel him urging me to follow the train of my unspoken thoughts even though he remained silent behind me.

"Why that one?" I asked aloud to no one in particular. "There are dozens of other far more valuable pieces in this room alone. Take this Monet for instance. Why take that one?"

Mr. Langley smiled at me again and I had the feeling of a schoolgirl who had raised her hand in class and gotten the answer right.

"I don't know," the curator confessed. There was a mild annoyance in his tone at being questioned by a woman but I chose to ignore it as I had my entire life. "Perhaps they liked it."

I turned on him, brow raised. "No one breaks into an art museum and steals a painting because they like it."

Mr. Langley scratched his chin and gazed down at the shattered glass once more.

"What is the name of the man who loaned you this paining?" Mr. Langley asked.

"Mr. Clyde Herbert," the curator answered. "I suppose I should be visiting him with the news."

"Not to worry. Miss Porter and I can tell him when we visit him."

"Visit him?"

"It was his painting," Mr. Langley saidnd it seems it was quite special to our thief if Miss Porter's knowledge of art valuation is correct and I have no reason to suspect it is not. Perhaps he has an indication of why this particular painting would have been stolen. Thank you for your time, Sir. I do hope you find a more adept night watchman to guard your precious art. Shall we, Miss Porter?"

Mr. Langley extended his arm and I took it. We turned and strode from the room, leaving the curator to attend to his remaining pieces. We passed back through the halls from which we had come and this time I allowed my eyes to wander.

"You know about art," Mr. Langley said. It was not phrased as a question but I could hear the curiosity in his tone all the same.

"I know as much about art as I do of any subject," I told him. "I've learned bits and pieces of various topics from binding books about them in my father's shop. He always used to get onto me for reading more than I bound."

Mr. Langley smiled at that.

"You know Monet," he said.

"Only that he is a famous artist. I have heard of him. I have not heard of Vincent Guillard. Therefore, that painting cannot be worth as much as a Monet."

Mr. Langley smiled at me.

"What?" I asked after an unnerving minute of that knowing smile.

"I thought you said you were not observant."

I rolled my eyes. "A fluke."

He chuckled at that.

"Though I'm not certain it mattered," I added. "We don't seem to be any closer to finding the culprit as we were before my brilliant observation."

"On the contrary," Mr. Langley said with a smile. We had reached the carriage outside of the museum now. The sunlight upon his golden hair made it shine in the bright London morning as he held open the door for me and offered a hand. "We may not know who stole the painting but we know who it was stolen from. What do you say to visiting Mr. Clyde Herbert?"

5 The Collector

■■■

Mr. Herbert's entry hall rivalled the London Museum of Art's in beauty. Every available space upon the ornate wood paneling was covered in beautiful renaissance paintings or sculpted busts of ancient philosophers. I had reigned in my wonder and curiosity at the museum when the old curator was leading us through the decorated halls but I saw no reason to show such restraint here in the foyer with no one present but a distracted Mr. Langley. I was admiring a particularly detailed sculpture of Socrates when the tall oaken doors at the end of the hall creaked open to reveal a balding middle aged man in the finest suit I had ever seen, black at the jacket and a deep plum purple at the lapel, a material that would have cost far more than a month's profits at my father's shop. He spared me the barest passing glance before his gaze settled onto my employer. Mr. Langley had not occupied himself with enjoying the displayed artwork around us as I had, choosing instead to focus on the massive clock hanging above us, a protruding bulb in the style of a London train station timepiece.

"Good morning, Mister..."

"Langley," Mr. Langley interjected in introduction, shaking the wealthy gentleman's hand as he did.

"Mr. Langley," Mr. Herbert repeated. "What can I do for you?"

"The curator at the museum sent me," Mr. Langley said. I glanced at him from my place near the wall. That was not entirely the truth. "I regret to inform you that your prized Guillard painting which you loaned the museum has been stolen."

Mr. Herbert's reaction was very strange. He seemed more disappointed than shocked. I was not the only one who noticed.

"You are not surprised?" my employer questioned.

"Unfortunately, no," Mr. Herbert said. "I had hoped the painting would be safer at the museum but it seems I was wrong."

"Safer," Mr. Langley repeated. "so you had reason to believe that someone might be trying to steal it?"

Mr. Herbert looked up at him then, his sorrow changing at once to suspicion as he narrowed his gaze.

"I'm sorry, Mr. Langley, I did not catch what you said your occupation was."

"No need to apologize," my employer answered jovially. "I did not disclose. I am an investigator with Scotland Yard, you see. I have been assigned the case of the stolen painting. You seem to know something of the theft?"

"I have another Guillard here in my house. I've added extra security since I heard of the others going missing."

"Others?"

Mr. Herbert looked rather uncomfortable all of a sudden. He cleared his throat and glanced around as if looking for an escape from Mr. Langley's poignant questions.

"How... how official of a capacity are you involved in Scotland Yard, Mr. Langley?" he asked.

"Fairly unofficial," my employer confessed. "In truth, I am more of a consulting private investigator whose services they have acquired to help find this art thief."

"I see. Well, you should know. Quite a few of these paintings have been stolen but many of the owners have not reported them missing due to the... not entirely legal way in which they were acquired."

Mr. Langley raised a brow at the confession.

"What do you mean?" he asked.

"Well, I was not aware of it at the time but it seems that... the auction that I bought these paintings at had not exactly verified the seller's authenticity."

"What do you mean?"

"The paintings were not being sold by the artist himself, you see. I mean, they couldn't be. Given what happened. But none of us knew at the time about that so we cannot be held responsible for purchasing something at auction that-"

"What do you mean 'given what happened'? Why couldn't the artist sell the paintings himself?"

Mr. Herbert glanced my way for the first time then. I had made my way over to them and stood only a few feet away from him next to Mr. Langley.

"It isn't... quite for a lady to hear."

I felt a faint hint of amusement at the wealthy Mr. Herbert referring to me as a lady but kept my comments to myself as Mr. Langley encouraged him.

"Miss Porter is my investigative partner," Mr. Langley told him. "I assure you. She can handle whatever it is that you have to say."

I fought the urge to look at my employer. Was he so certain I could? Did he not consider me a lady? Of course he didn't, I scolded myself. He knew better.

"Well, Mr. Guillard was quite unable to sell his own works after his... well, after his suicide, you see."

I felt my hands fly up to cover my open mouth. How dreadful.

"Suicide?" Mr. Langley asked curiously. "When was this?"

"A couple of weeks ago," Mr. Herbert answered, looking apologetically my way. But I had recovered quickly enough and my mind had moved on to another conundrum. Mr. Langley had not known about Mr. Guillard's suicide which meant that it likely was not in the police file he had been given which meant that we were wasting our time unless there was something specifically tying Mr. Guillard to this string of stolen paintings and if that were the case than this was, perhaps, an entirely different investigation and we should be approaching it in another way.

"Mr. Herbert," I began and he smiled kindly at me. "You said that you heightened your security once you learned that many of your friends had their paintings stolen?"

"Yes, dear," he answered. I tried to ignore the condescension.

"Were those paintings Guillards?"

"Yes."

"All of them?" Mr. Langley interjected, his curiosity getting the best of him when he realized what I had intended with my line of questioning. Mr. Herbert paused for a moment to think but then nodded.

"Yes, all of them."

"Mr. Herbert, do you recall who it was that put those paintings up for auction?"

"I do indeed. A fellow by the name of Louis Dubois. He was a friend of Vincent Guillard's, claimed to have had his permission to sell his works. Though we found out afterwards that was not the case."

"How did you find that out?"

"One of the men who had been at the auction read about Mr. Guillard's suicide in the paper and put it together that the paintings had to have been sold after the death of the artist which seemed quite odd. We went to the treasurer of the auction who confronted Mr. Dubois and he confessed that Mr. Guillard had never given him express permission to sell his work. It was too late by then, though, you see. Because the paintings had been sold and the money collected."

Mr. Langley nodded and bit his lip, brow creased in concentration. Mr. Herbert seemed to be waiting for him to continue the conversation, fidgeting nervously after his admission that he had purchased stolen art, but my employer seemed lost in thought. I could tell that Mr. Herbert felt guilty about his role in the illegal sale though I quite agreed with him that it was no fault of his own if he truly hadn't the slightest idea that the work had not been sold with the permission of the artist. Mr. Langley did not seem eager to assuage our host's guilt, however, choosing to remain in thoughtful silence and stare up at that strange clock once more. After a few moments of awkward silence, I decided to break the tension with a request of my own. "You said you still had one of the paintings here?"

"Yes," Mr. Herbert answered with another condescending smile though this time paired with a gratitude for my intervention. He was conversing with me as though I were no more than a school aged child and, though it irked me, it did not surprise me. Given Mr. Herbert's superior dress and exquisite choice in décor, he was well aware of what wealth looked like and, though I was wearing one of my sister's finest dresses, he knew that I was no higher than the merchant class and must have guessed me to be uneducated as well. I was long past bristling at such assumptions seeing as they were made by every passing member of the gentry I had ever met. I had resigned myself to a fate of condescension and pretentiousness.

"Could we see it?"

Mr. Langley looked up at that and Mr. Herbert glanced between us as if surmising whether or not we could be a threat to his precious painting. After a minute, he relented. "Very well. Follow me."

We did. He led us up to the second floor landing and into an office. The painting hung on proud display behind a large mahogany desk not unlike the one in Mr. Langley's own office. The painting itself was exquisite. It was of a scene at a busy park. Mothers whispered to one another and children played. Men laughed and someone had brought a dog. It was a very happy scene indeed and one wrought in the brightest paints available. It was a marvel that someone who had painted such a jubilant scene could be found dead at his own hands. I approached it carefully, letting my eyes rove over the exquisite detail, taking in the gradient shading and the small embellishments. It seemed that the longer one looked at the painting, more of the scene revealed itself.

I was not sure why I had asked to see it, only that I felt that I should. If someone was so intent on stealing this particular artist's paintings then it did not feel as though we could ever truly understand such motivation having never seen one of the works ourselves. It seemed necessary that we had viewed one with our own eyes and, now that I had, I could see how this art could inspire envy. It was incredible. I could see why this artist's works had found success at auction and I could see why someone would want to sell them. As for why someone would want to steal them, I felt that that particular motivation was not held within the colors themselves.

"It's my wife's favorite," Mr. Herbert said suddenly, pleased with my admiration of the art.

"I can see why," I told him. "It's beautiful."

"You are an appreciator of the arts, are you Miss Porter?"

"I do enjoy a skilled artist's work," I answered. "I appreciate those who have the gift to create beauty from nothing."

He beamed at my answer. "An enlightened response. I quite agree myself. What is the use in having all of this money if I cannot spend it on that which I enjoy? My wife is of quite the same opinion as you. That artists create beauty."

I caught Mr. Langley's eye from behind Mr. Herbert. He gestured for me to keep the man talking as I had seemed to have gained his trust. The condescension was gone from his tone and replaced instead by that fervent friendly eagerness which drove the tone of a man who had discovered a kindred spirit, someone with whom he shared a particular interest. I could admit that I knew very little of the world of art itself but had always admired the beauty of such creations and knew enough to, at the very least, praise an excellent painting when I saw one. Besides, what I was truly saying was no more than common flattery and all men, wealthy or not, always responded to flattery.

"Your wife seems quite the tasteful woman," I told him and he beamed once more.

"Indeed," he agreed. "Much like yourself, I imagine. I suppose that is why you are assisting Mr. Langley on this case?"

"Someone must remind him of his manners."

Mr. Herbert let out a booming laugh at that. I risked a smile and noticed that Mr. Langley was smiling back at me, eyebrow raised at the barb.

"Mr. Herbert," I said then, touching the man's arm gently as he calmed himself. "Would it be too much trouble to request a list of those acquaintances of yours who purchased Guillard paintings at the same auction? If they are encountering theft by the same thief, their experiences could be quite useful in establishing a pattern and ultimately solving this case."

"Of course, dear," Mr. Herbert exclaimed happily and then, crossing behind his desk, he retrieved a pen and paper and began writing down the names and addresses of all those acquaintances whom he could remember had purchased a Guillard painting, circling those whom had had theirs stolen. In the end, it seemed that many more paintings had been stolen than the police had record of. Mr. Herbert claimed it was likely that many of the men had not reported their paintings stolen so as not to draw attention to the "less than legal" way in which they had been acquired. In the end, we thanked Mr. Herbert profusely and headed out of his house and into the carriage with a tangible list of potential leads. I found myself feeling much more accomplished as I settled in for the ride back to Mr. Langley's residence for lunch. Gripping the list in my hands, I looked up to see Mr. Langley smiling at me.

"What?" I asked.

"I had no idea you were so accomplished in flattery," he told me. "Perhaps I was right to choose a woman as my investigative partner. Men respond far better to the flirtation of a beautiful young woman than they do to the questioning of an authoritative man. Is that how you beguiled your way into my employment, Miss Porter? Flirtation?"

Trying to ignore the teasing tone of his voice and the fact that he had just called me a beautiful young woman, I answered simply. "When I am flirting with you, Mr. Langley, I assure you, you will know."

Mr. Langley chuckled at that and busied himself with watching the hectic London streets fade away outside the window as we drove on. I gazed down at the list in my hands and wondered where we should begin. Most likely with the ones who had a painting stolen as well. There would be a crime scene of sorts to investigate there. Perhaps even some physical evidence if we were lucky. Maybe even some indication of why these paintings were being targeted in such a way. I was so absorbed in my thoughts that I didn't realize we had arrived back at Mr. Langley's house until he was helping me out of the carriage. I tucked the list away in my bag and followed him into the house, handing my hat and gloves to Bernard as he greeted us.

"Lunch has been prepared, Sir," Bernard informed us. "It is waiting for you in the dining room. Miss Langley is there now."

"Excellent, Bernard, thank you. Miss Porter, would you care to join us for lunch?"

I smiled. "I would be honored."

I followed Mr. Langley across the hall and into the dining room. Miss Langley beamed at me as I entered, positively bouncing on her toes with giddiness at the sight of me.

"Charlotte!" she squealed. "Do sit next to me. I can't wait to hear about your morning."

I smiled, unable to stop myself. Her bubbly happiness was contagious. I took a seat next to Miss Langley and across the table from her brother as a kindly young woman placed our meals in front of us. I smiled up at her and nodded a thanks. She smiled back and patted me briefly on the shoulder as she returned to the kitchen. I made a note to learn her name at my earliest convenience.

"Tell me all about the investigation," Miss Langley gushed.

"You want to hear about the investigation?" Mr. Langley asked, surprised. "You never ask me about my investigations."

"And I'm not asking you now," she snapped and I could not keep the smirk from my lips. Mr. Langley noticed it and shook his head, a playful smile of his own distorting his handsome features.

"It's been going rather well so far," I answered her question. "We've made significant progress already in my opinion. And Mr. Herbert gave us a list of potential leads and witnesses to speak to which was very—"

"Mr. Herbert?" Miss Langley inquireds in Mr. Clyde Herbert?"

"You know him?" I asked with interest.

"Hardly. I know his daughter. Elizabeth Herbert. You know her, Alexander."

"Do I?" he asked, clearly more interested in his soup than the mention of his sister's friend.

"Don't be such a dolt, Alexander. You've met her on more than one occasion."

"Forgive me," he said, a hint of exhaustion in his voice. "There are simply so many Elizabeths in London."

I smiled at that and told him. "My sister's name is Elizabeth. Though we all call her Liza."

He smiled up at me. "You have a sister?"

"Two. Though I imagine if commonality is a hot button issue for you, you won't care for my elder sister's name either."

"What is it?"

"Victoria."

He smirked at that.

"Anyway," Miss Langley interrupted, clearly impatient with our conversation. "I suppose I cannot fault you for not remembering Elizabeth Herbert, Alexander. She is rather unremarkable and quite dull if I'm being honest."

"Elena," Mr. Langley warned though it was halfhearted at best and did nothing to change Miss Langley's speech. I doubted he could keep his sister from expressing her opinion even if he sincerely wished to. She seemed a headstrong one, this Miss Langley.

"Why did you go to visit Mr. Herbert?" Miss Langley asked me.

"Oh, well we were investigating a stolen painting at the London Museum of Art and it turned out to be on loan from his private collection," I answered.

"Oh yes. Mr. Herbert's private collection," she repeated with a roll of her eyes. "Every time I see Elizabeth, she's on about one of his newest pieces. The man has an obsession. Do you enjoy art, Charlotte?"

"Indeed she does," Mr. Langley answered before I could. I glanced up to see him smirking at me. He was incorrigible, wasn't he?

"Really?" Miss Langley gasped. "All sorts? Not just paintings and sculptures?"

"I'm not sure what you-" but I didn't get to finish.

"Do you like the theater, Charlotte?"

I stared at Miss Langley for a moment.

"I- well, I'm not certain," I told her. "I've never been."

She gasped. "You have to go! You would absolutely adore it. Oh, I'll take you! This Friday! We will take in a show together. Doesn't that sound fun?"

I glanced at Mr. Langley who seemed rather preoccupied with his soup all of a sudden. I would be getting no help from him, it seemed.

"Yes," I said then because there was nothing else I could say and Miss Langley squealed with delight.

"Wonderful! I'm thrilled. Alexander, do pick up two tickets to the theater for Miss Porter and I while you're out and about."

He nodded without looking up and Miss Langley fell into an in depth history of every show she had ever attended along with the aspects that she felt I would enjoy and those that I would not. Luckily, her rambling allowed me to finish eating my meal without having to add much more to the conversation than the occasional hum of agreement. Though it gave me time to think, I could not help but wonder what a girl like me should wear to the theater. I had no ornate dresses like Miss Langley's to boast of. I supposed one of my old church dresses would have to do. Though they hadn't seen the light of day since my mother's passing.

"If you'll excuse us, Elena," Mr. Langley said, interrupting one of Miss Langley's rants about a particular play she had seen the previous spring and tossing down his napkin and standing. "Miss Porter and I have some more business to attend to this afternoon. Miss Porter?"

I nodded and stood as Mr. Langley left the room. When he was gone, I turned to his sister.

"Thank you for your kindness," I told her with a smile. "I am eager to attend the theater with you and I appreciate the invitation."

She smiled back at me as I took my leave. I met Mr. Langley in the foyer and took my hat and gloves from Bernard at the door, donning them as we stepped back out into the warm London day.

"I want to apologize for Elena," he said as we strode toward the carriage. "She can be rather... pushy."

"Well, as all I perceive her to be pushing me toward is friendship, I have no qualms with it," I answered and he nodded at that but his expression betrayed a different emotion altogether, a strange emotion. Perhaps my eyes deceived me but it almost appeared to be relief.

After a short ride to the London police station and a quick conversation with a detective on duty there, Mr. Langley and I found ourselves in a very large records room surrounded by filing cabinets and flickering lights. We were sitting at a long wooden table, each of us bent over a stack of police reports, file folders and loose papers filling the space of the desk between us. Mr. Langley had requested any record of incident involving a stolen painting whose artist had been one Vincent Guillard brought to us and there were at least half a dozen to review. The number was far lower than that which Mr. Herbert had given us but I knew that a lot of the thefts would not have been reported and we would only have the collector's memory to rely upon for those.

We spent hours poring over the case files, comparing each report for similarities and examining them individually for oddities. When we had completed our review of the thefts and my notes on the subject had been exhausted, Mr. Langley requested the report of Mr. Guillard's suicide and we reviewed that as well. I had worried, before hand, if I had the stomach for investigating such a matter but it proved relatively easy for me to view the case objectively. Though that could have been because these descriptions and details were in print and not in front of me. The coroner's report was what I had been dreading the most but found myself surprised at my composure as Mr. Langley read it aloud, feet kicked up on the desk in front of him, one hand lifted behind his head, rubbing his sore neck. I paced on the opposite side of the table, walking to and fro, allowing my tired eyes to glance about my surroundings without taking much of them in as my listening focused in on the words Mr. Langley was saying. After the coroner's report came the report of the scene itself.

We had been in the process of deciphering the notes of the first officer who had arrived at the scene when I felt myself beginning to yawn. I did my best to suppress it but to no avail. Mr. Langley noticed easily enough seeing as I was leaning over him at the time to view the file over his shoulder. He seemed to snap out of a trance. He blinked a few times and turned to look at the clock behind me. Then he gasped and began to gather the folders back into a neat pile.

"Goodness it's nearly midnight," he exclaimed and I turned, in disbelief, to view the clock myself. I was surprised to find that he had been correct. It was nearly midnight. I stared at him as he packed everything away, amazed that time had slipped away from us so quickly, astonished at how entranced I had been by the gruesome work. The work that I had been so sure I would not have a penchant for.

I helped Mr. Langley finish packing up the case files and return them to the desk clerk and then the two of us walked, arm in arm, from the police station and onto the street. It was far emptier at this hour than it had been when we had entered and we found the carriage driver asleep at his post. Mr. Langley gently roused him and then turned to me.

"What is your address?" he asked.

"What?" I responded.

"There is no way I am going to let you walk home at this hour, Miss Porter. Please, allow my driver to take you home."

I gave him my address and climbed in the back of the carriage with Mr. Langley. It was a quiet drive as we each fell into silence driven by either exhaustion or contemplation. For me, it was exhaustion but I suspected, due to the new light in his bright blue eyes, that it was the opposite for him. It was not long at all before the carriage was coming to a stop and Mr. Langley emerged to assist me down. As my hand grasped his, I saw movement in the window above and glanced up to see Liza gazing down at us, a look of utter shock on her face. I hadn't had the time or the forethought to consider what sort of response such a scene would illicit and now I found myself nearly regretting accepting his offer to see me home. I would, undoubtedly, have many questions to answer for this in the morning.

"Liza?" Mr. Langley guessed and I turned to see him looking up at my sister, a smile on his face. He offered a wave as I stepped onto the pavement and my sister, wide eyed, dropped the curtain and jumped away. He chuckled.

"She isn't used to such an escort," I told him. "Nor am I."

"It's the least I could do. I sincerely apologize for the late hour, Miss Porter."

I waved him off.

"Occupational hazard," I answered, stifling another yawn as I made my way to the door. "Goodnight Mr. Langley."

"Goodnight Miss Porter."

6 Obstruction

The moment the door to my sister's residence closed behind me, Liza was at my side, smiling up at me like a child who had just received her first piece of candy. The apartment itself was still and dark, all members of the family having retired long ago. At least, I would not have to face my eldest sister tonight. Her tirade would wait until the morning when I've had my rest and, hopefully, my breakfast. For now, I only had to face the curiosity and willful imagination of my younger sister who had seen me dropped at the door by a friendly, wealthy gentleman whom she had never before met.

"What?" I asked her, too exhausted to come up with anything more than that. I yawned and stretched as I made my way to the pallet that we shared in the living room. She bounded after me like a lost puppy and sat cross legged on the floor as I settled in, electing not to undress for the night but rather to sleep in the dress and worry about my appearance in the morning.

"That was your boss?" she asked and I nodded. "You didn't say he was so handsome!"

"Is he?"

She made a loud noise that sounded like all of the air had been expelled from her lungs at once.

"Do not try to pretend that you haven't noticed, Charlotte," she chastised. "You'd have to be blind not to."

I sighed at that. Typically I would be rather inclined to indulge Liza's girlish fantasies. Victoria and I had always tried our hardest to allow her a child's whimsy but, at the very moment, I was too exhausted to listen to this.

"You know how the world works, Liza," I answered her, yawning as I placed my head upon my pillow. "What would it matter even if I did think he was handsome?"

And then the world faded to black and I fell easily into a much anticipated slumber.

The next morning, I awoke to an irritated Victoria and a wary Liza. Apparently, my younger sister had not cared greatly for my hopeless remark the night before and my older sister had not cared for my coming home so late at all or any indication of whatever scandal she was certain the neighbors had cooked up since. She eyed me all morning and I had just chosen to ignore it when she finally spoke up.

"Is this to be a regular occurrence?" she asked all of a sudden, placing a hand on her hips and peering at me over the pan of eggs in her hand as she did. Both my father and Benjamin stopped eating and looked up at us.

"I'm not sure I know what you mean," I said as innocently as I could, holding my head high and scooping another helping of eggs onto my plate to continue my act of disinterest. Victoria sighed loudly.

"The coming home at all hours of the night," she clarified. "Benjamin and I have to be up very early to operate the shop and if you are going to disturb us-"

"I wasn't aware I had woken you," I grumbled. "I'll try to be quieter next time."

"Next time?" the question came from Benjamin this time. I glanced up at him in surprise. Typically, he was on my side. He seemed to sense my confusion at this turn and changed his tone to be as gentle as it could. I found it condescending. "Charlotte, you are a grown woman and you are free to make your own choices but you must think of your... reputation. If the neighbors were to see you coming home at midnight, helped out of a carriage by some unmarried gentleman-"

"Even the neighbors are not awake at midnight!" Charlotte shouted. Ben closed his eyes as if trying to maintain his composure but mine was already lost. I jumped to my feet, face reddening and hands shaking.

"You are my family. You know that what exists between Mr. Langley and I is purely business. I should not have to explain myself to you. You all know exactly why I need this job and why we need the money. So if it's my reputation that you are so worried about, perhaps you should all start contributing a bit more to our father's debts so that I will not have to remain in Mr. Langley's employment for long and I can return here and sit around all day waiting for a man to waltz through that door and marry me since that seems to be of the utmost importance to you, sister."

With that, I grabbed my bag, hat, and gloves, and stormed out of the apartment. I was still fuming by the time I had called a cab and still smoldering by the time I had reached Mr. Langley's door. He was already outside again this morning, ready for wherever this day would take us. He helped me out of my cab and into his carriage and sat across from me. I had returned his morning wishes with some of my own but they had been muttered through gritted teeth and I would be a fool to think he hadn't noticed.

I had wanted to ask Mr. Langley where we were going but I was afraid that, if I opened my mouth, some of my anger at my family would slip out at him. So I kept my lips clenched shut and gazed out the window as we rode. I felt his gaze fall on me from time to time but he mainly kept his attention on the case file in his lap and neither of us spoke much as we rode. When the carriage stopped, Mr. Langley helped me out and I saw that we were back at the police station. I mentally prepared myself for a day of rifling through even more case files but I was surprised when Mr. Langley led us, not to the file room in the back but to the head detective's office in the front.

"Ryland," Mr. Langley called in jovial greeting as we entered the office. The man behind the desk looked up and broke into a smile. He was not young but he was not as old as I would have expected the head detective of Scotland Yard to be either. His hair was mostly brown with only faint patches of grey here or there. I estimated him to be in his mid-forties. He stood from his seat and shook Mr. Langley's hand before casting me a smile.

"Langley," he greeted warmly. "Miss Porter. To what do I owe such a pleasure?"

I was shocked that he knew my name. He had not been at the station the proceeding day when Mr. Langley and I had confined ourselves to the records room in our search for connections to our case. As far as I knew, I had never met this man in person, only heard of his investigation intersecting ours from the witnesses we spoke to. But he seemed to know of me. Perhaps Mr. Langley had informed him that I too would be working the case. That would have been sensible of him, putting my name on whatever official list seemed to get him into so many places and privileges.

"We would like to speak with the detectives who were at the Guillard suicide scene," Mr. Langley told him. Chief Detective Ryland studied my employer carefully for a moment. Then leaned against his desk and narrowed his eyes.

"Why?" he asked.

"All of the paintings that were stolen were Guillard's. We have reason to believe his suicide may be connected to our case. I cannot give you any more information than that as I do not have it myself. Not until I speak with your men."

Mr. Langley smiled. The Chief Detective considered this for a moment and then finally nodded and returned to his desk.

"Very well. I'll gather them in Benson's old office. You can speak with them there."

Mr. Langley thanked the Chief Detective and then escorted me out of his office and into an empty office across the hall. He offered me the only chair and I thanked him and took my seat. Mr. Langley himself leaned against the wall to my right and waited for the men to enter. After a few moments, three of them filed in. Two detectives and an officer. Both detectives seemed quite experienced with matching grey hair and worn suits. The officer was very young and seemed nervous at being placed in a room with his superiors. His eyes met mine the moment he entered and I could tell that I was a curiosity for him. A woman in a police station who wasn't a victim. It was not a sight he was accustomed to and I am sure it only served to heighten his already strained nerves.

"Gentlemen," Mr. Langley began when they had entered, being far too generous with the title in my opinion. "I would like to question you on the suicide of Mr. Vincent Guillard. Ryland says you were all there at some point."

"We were," one of the detectives, the more heavy set one, grunted.

"Excellent," Mr. Langley said. "Would you mind explaining the scene as you found it?"

The officer opened his mouth but the detective beat him to it.

"He was in his studio," the detective answered. "Sitting at his desk. There was an open bottle of pills next to him, spilled out over the table. His head was on the desk and the note was under his hand. He must have still been writing it when he died because the pen was still in his hand. There were paintings all over the place, some of them finished, some not."

"There was a note? Do you recall what it said?"

"Not exactly. Just the typical tortured artist stuff. No one would appreciate him in his time and all that. York wrote down what it said, didn't you?"

"I did," the other detective, York, answered. "Got a copy of it at my desk. I can get that for you if you need it."

"I would appreciate that very much," Mr. Langley said. "You said he was still writing the note when he perished?"

"Best guess," the first detective shrugged. "Still had the pen in his hand so I imagine."

"But the note was finished? It had come to a natural end?"

"It had. Signed it and all."

Mr. Langley nodded and I watched him, hoping that I was thinking the same thing that he was. If the note was finished and signed, why did Mr. Guillard still hold the pen in his hand by the time they found him? And why would he have taken the life ending pills before he began to write his note? It seemed to be a very strange scene that these detectives had encountered. At least, I thought so. They did not seem particularly disturbed by it and I wondered why that was. Had they investigated so many deaths that they had become desensitized to it? Were the detectives of the Scotland Yard as lazy as the local constabularies? I hoped not. It did not bode well for my current employment if that were the case.

"Who called it in?" Mr. Langley asked. "Who reported the suicide?"

"The friend," York answered and then turned to his companion. "You remember that fellow?"

"Oh yeah, the gentleman," the other detective recalled, rubbing his beard as he did. "He was a friend of the artist's. He had dropped in for a social call and found him like that. Poor man was distraught. We could hardly get a sensible word out of him. He kept saying something about the paintings. What was it?"

"That he wouldn't allow us to wreck them with our rifling," York answered, sneering at the indication that their professional police work might be considered no more than rifling. "Said he knew how we ransacked places for the sake of our investigation and he wouldn't let the paintings be spoiled. He took them."

"He took them?" Mr. Langley sat up straighter. "Do you remember the gentleman's name?"

"Dubois, I believe. Funny French name."

Mr. Langley glanced my way and I gave him a tiny nod to show that I understood. It was the same name that Mr. Herbert had given us before, the name of the man who had auctioned the paintings off without telling anyone that he did not have permission to do so. Now we knew how he had come into possession of them.

"Do you know what he did with the paintings?" Mr. Langley asked.

"Sold them most likely," York answered with a shrug.

"You assume he sold them but you did not do anything to stop him? Isn't it against the law for a man to sell another man's work for profit?"

"It is," the first detective said. "But we've got far too much on our plate to chase down some gentleman for selling his dead friend's artwork."

"Did you interview Mr. Dubois for the stolen painting case?"

"What for? If he really was the one who sold them, why would he steal them back?"

Why, indeed.

"Why are you investigating a suicide anyway?" the heavy set detective questioned, his pudgy eyes narrowing in suspicion for the first time. It appeared that Mr. Langley had irritated them with the obvious insinuation his questions inspired that they were not doing their jobs properly. "It's an open and shut case. There was nothing strange about the scene and I can't see how the death of an artist has anything to do with his paintings being stolen. Hate to say it, Langley, but I think you're barking up the wrong tree on this one. Now, if you don't mind, York and I have some real cases that need working on. We'll get you that suicide note but I think you need to shift your focus back to the case at hand."

With that, the detectives left the office, leaving us alone with the fresh faced officer. Mr. Langley seemed slightly put off by the admonishment he had just received from a man far inferior to his own standing. His brows were creased in that familiar way that I had already come to know meant he was lost in thought. I knew how fragile men's egos could be and I doubted that trying to converse with him at present would result in anything other than curt words and hurt feelings. So I turned my attention elsewhere. He had completely forgotten about the officer as a man bred into his class was likely to do. But I hadn't. I smiled warmly at him.

"What's your name?" I asked sweetly and Mr. Langley came out of his reverie long enough to look from me to the officer, blinking at him momentarily as though remembering all at once that he was in the room.

"Thomas, ma'am," He spoke as though all of his anxieties were pressed into his voice. "Thomas Umber."

"Well, Mr. Umber, were you present at the scene?"

"I was the first officer to respond to the scene. It was me who fetched Detective York and Detective Higgins."

Mr. Langley's hand fell away from his face as he gazed at the boy, renewed interest peaked. I settled back into my seat as Mr. Langley's eyes bore into him, knowing that I had accomplished what I had set about to and that Mr. Langley would attend to the questioning now. Perhaps I was here more to steer him in the directions he may not himself consider than to make observations and investigate myself.

"Did you see anything strange about the scene?" he asked. The boy looked from Mr. Langley to me and then out of the pane of glass separating us from the rest of the police force. He seemed to be weighing his options, deciding whether or not he should tell us whatever it was that he had seen.

"The detectives have already decided this is a closed case," he said quietly, betraying the root of his concern. I glanced out of the glass where the older detectives were standing near their own desks. Their eyes strayed to us from time to time but they were seemingly lost in their own conversation about whatever new case had recently crossed their desks and did not seem all that concerned about what the young officer might be disclosing to us.

"What you tell us will not leave this room," Mr. Langley promised. "We won't tell them. If your information leads us to some conclusion than you can choose whether or not you would like your name attributed to it. But, for the time being, you can trust that we will not tell anyone where our information came from."

The young officer looked from Mr. Langley to me and then relaxed his shoulders and faced the man again.

"I noticed that the pen was in Mr. Guillard's right hand," he confessed. Mr. Langley looked to me to see if I had understood the significance of this revelation. Unfortunately, I had not.

"And?"

"And it was well-known that Mr. Guillard was left handed."

Mr. Langley's gaze snapped back to me and I felt my jaw go slack in surprise. This was quite the revelation indeed. Not only had it seemed odd that a man had finished his suicide note and yet continued to clutch the pen as he was dying but now there was an indication that he hadn't written the note at all. There would be no reason that I could see for Mr. Guillard to write such an important note with his non-dominant hand. And it would be common for people to notice the rarity of a left-handed artist so we could trust in the reports that he was, in fact, left handed. I saw no reason for that to be a lie either.

"Thank you very much, Mr. Umber," I said as sweetly as I could manage, standing from my place on the chair and walking cautiously toward him. I placed a reaffirming hand on his shoulder and guided him to the door. "You have been an asset to our investigation."

He smiled at me sheepishly, color blossoming on his youthful round cheeks, before leaving the room. Mr. Langley turned to me once we were alone.

"Are you thinking what I'm thinking?" he asked.

"That our stolen art case just got much more complicated?" I asked and he smiled.

"Indeed, it did. I think that perhaps we should pay this Mr. Dubois we have heard so much about a visit."

I nodded in agreement and rose from my seat. After saying a friendly goodbye to Chief Detective Ryland and collecting the promised copy of the artist's suicide note from the irritated detectives, Mr. Langley led me out to the carriage and helped me inside. He had gotten Mr. Dubois's address from the case file we had looked over on Mr. Guillard's suicide and he gave it to the driver before joining me in the carriage. We discussed the case as we drove, speaking aloud the questions we had both asked ourselves through the course of our interview with the police but, with no new information, it served only to ensure that we were on the same page.

We arrived at Mr. Dubois' home sometime later. I emerged from the carriage to find myself standing in front of the most beautiful palatial mansion I had ever seen. It was three times the size of Mr. Langley's manor though with half the charm. Everything was made of marble or gold in designs so intricate and elegant that they bordered on the ridiculous. The whole house had an air of being the most expensive thing that one would ever see and wanting you to know it. I did. And found myself rather unimpressed. A servant greeted us before my feet had even hit the pavement. When Mr. Langley disclosed who we were and the reason for our visit, that of course being that we were working with the police to solve a random string of art thefts, the servant bustled off to inform his master of our arrival.

We were led, by another butler present, into the foyer of the home. The ceilings were at least twenty feet above me and I marveled up at them as the butler took our hats and scarves. As unimpressed by the golden exterior as I was, I found myself quite interested in the architecture of the domed hall we entered. It was a work of art itself and, though undoubtedly designed for the same premise of shock and awe, I could not help but admire it all the same. Mr. Dubois himself joined us soon after we entered, coming down the ornate spiral staircase on one side of the room with a welcoming smile and a hand running through his disheveled black hair. He was quite attractive, I noticed, and wondered for the first time if he were all alone in this giant home.

"Good morning Mr. Langley," he said as he descended to greet us. "And Miss Porter."

He smiled at me as he approached, welcoming us by the names that we had given the servant who had undoubtedly told him. He took my hand and kissed it for so long that Mr. Langley had to clear his throat before he would return his gaze to him though not before gazing up at me from beneath those thick lashes of his. As clearly flirtatious as the action was, there was something about it, something that seemed to mimic the same level of pageantry reflected in the elaborate décor surrounding us.

"What can I do for you?" Mr. Dubois asked pleasantly, breezing past the awkwardness which had just unfolded as though it had never occurred. "My servant said you were with the police?"

"In an unofficial capacity," Mr. Langley answered. "They have retained our services to investigate a painting that was stolen from the London Museum of Art."

"I see. That's terrible. I'm not certain I see how such an investigation brought you to my door, however. Would you care for some tea? Miss Porter?"

"Oh, that would be lovely," I answered and he smiled and clapped at a nearby maid who hurried off to fetch the beverage. He walked away then, leaving us to follow. We did. Though Mr. Langley grumbled at the rudeness. I hardly noticed it. I supposed I was used to the wealthy behaving as they pleased around me. Mr. Dubois led us into his drawing room and sat as the maid poured our tea. I thanked her as I took my cup and peered at the elegant artwork adorning the walls of the room. As the drawing room was the traditional place to welcome and entertain guests and visitors, it was typically the most beautifully decorated room in the house. Though this room paled in comparison to the grandeur of the domed foyer, it had its own element of charm just the same. The artwork here was more personal with scenes depicting the London social elite and even royalty. There were antiques adorning the shelves as well and, in a far corner, stood a pedestal with a glass encasing on top. Within the glass was a large, ancient Bible, opened to a particular page. I could see the exquisite detail of the sacred text from my seat and fought against the urge to run for it. Art and books. My weaknesses combined.

"It seems the painting that was stolen was painted by the late Vincent Guillard," Mr. Langley told him then, returning to the point and refocusing my attention. "We are told Mr. Guillard was a friend of yours?"

Mr. Dubois's expression changed from polite, friendly welcoming to the sorrowful face of a man still in mourning. He set his tea down and sighed. I felt a pang in my chest at having caused him pain in his grief and wished that I hadn't been so distracted by the Bible in the corner. I could have phrased such a question a bit more tactfully had I been more aware of my employer's intentions.

"Yes," he told us. "A very good friend."

"We are hoping that you can tell us a little about your friend," Mr. Langley continued. "Did he have any enemies?"

"Everyone positively loved Vincent. He was the life of every party, never to know a stranger. He was absolutely adored. I cannot think of anyone who ever spoke an ill word of him."

"Do you know of any reason why someone may want to steal his art?"

"Well, he was brilliant," Mr. Dubois told us with a sad smile. "His work was utter perfection, beautiful. And worth quite a bit as well."

"But worth more due to his untimely death, yes?"

I felt my jaw drop at Mr. Langley's boldness. This man was in grief. This was no time to speak so harshly. Mr. Dubois just raised a brow in confusion, the grace bred so well into him that the only indication of his annoyance at such a suggestion was the slight, faint twitching of his left eyebrow.

"I suppose that for a brief period of time once Vincent was found dead the art sold for a higher price. Why do you-"

"And you sold them, didn't you?"

Mr. Dubois's gaze shifted to me but I did not see the horror in his expression that I had expected. Rather, I saw discomfort. That was intriguing.

"I took possession of them during the police investigation into Vincent's death. I kept them for some time in my home but they brought me too much sadness so I had to rid myself of them. I'm not certain what that has to do with a stolen painting or what you are implying but-"

"Where does one sell artwork illegally?"

"Pardon me?"

"It was illegal. They were not your paintings to sell."

Mr. Dubois looked downright nervous now. He glanced from Mr. Langley to me and back again before he finally released a breath.

"Are you going to arrest me?" he asked.

"I told you, I am not a detective," Mr. Langley smiled and said. "My work for the police is unofficial. In fact, I am a man of means myself. I simply came across your name in this case and wondered where one could buy illegal artwork. Of course, I would be asking for a friend."

So that was his tactic. Mr. Dubois's nerves vanished in an instant, replaced by a knowing and mischievous smile.

"There is an auction house in a less reputable part of London," Mr. Dubois told Mr. Langley easily now that he believed my gentleman employer to be a co-conspirator. "They will sell anything so long as their cut is large enough. For that reason, it draws a much... wealthier crowd."

Mr. Langley leaned forward to show interest and I found myself admiring his capacity for acting. Should his investments and investigations not work out, the man could have quite the career in the theater. I abandoned the thought almost at once for fear of giggling at the thought of Mr. Langley, in costume, reciting a sonnet to some actress and ruining his plan. It seemed to be working, however. Mr. Dubois leaned forward in his chair and peered about him as though there might be a constable lurking in the shadows of his own home and forgetting, apparently, that he was already speaking to someone with far more power than a local constable.

"There is one tonight actually," Mr. Dubois practically whispered. "I had intended to go myself. I would be happy to introduce you to the regulars, Mr. Langley, if you are interested. I am not certain quite what you are looking for but I'm certain these men will know where to find it."

Mr. Langley raised a brow and sat back in his chair, smiling and thinking as if considering Mr. Dubois's offer.

"That would be wonderful," he said at last. "I would appreciate the address, Mr. Dubois."

Mr. Dubois retrieved a pen and paper to write down the address and, as he did, I caught Mr. Langley's eye. He gave me a wink that sent an unexplained thrill through my jangled nerves and then turned back to Mr. Dubois just as he approached with the note. Mr. Langley took the paper and stood. I got to my feet as well.

"Thank you very much for your time Mr. Dubois," Mr. Langley said, heading for the door. "I imagine we will be seeing each other again soon."

I followed Mr. Langley out of the drawing room and to the door where the butler who had helped us inside before handed us our hats and gloves as Mr. Dubois bid us goodbye with that pleasant smile upon his face once more. He had already turned off and headed back up the stairs from whence he had come by the time the door closed behind us and we were walking back to our carriage.

"I do hope you don't have any plans this evening, Miss Porter," Mr. Langley said as he helped me, once more, into the carriage. "Because I'm afraid you will be working late again."

"I would like to stop in to warn my sisters that I will be returning home late again tonight if at all possible," I said a few moments later. Mr. Langley and I were back in his carriage as it jostled it's way down the wealthy London lane on its way to another. Mr. Langley looked up at me then. He had been focused on Mr. Guillard's suicide note which he held in his hands so intently that I thought perhaps he might not have heard me and I had begun to repeat myself when he answered.

"Of course," he replied. "We can stop by on our way into town."

I sat back then and allowed him to continue his studious examination of the curious note, watching as his bright eyes darted over the page, lips moving in some sort of muttered trance. After a moment of silence, however, I grew restless and could hold my tongue no longer.

"What do you make of it?" I asked, nodding my head at the letter in his hands.

"Detective Higgins was right. It seems to be textbook tortured artist. He goes on about how the world never appreciated his work in life and how they will appreciate it more in death. Then there's the bit about how no one properly values art any longer. It's quite the tirade for a suicide note. It would be better suited as a manifesto if you ask me."

He handed me the note and I read, eyes darting over the page. There was even more on the back. Mr. Langley was right. This was rather lengthy for a suicide note. And curiously made no mention of friends or family or any comfort to them as a suicide note usually did. It also mentioned no specific reason for the supposed act other than unappreciation and a devalued sense of self-worth. The handwriting was neat, too neat to have been done by the non-dominant hand. It lacked the usual smudges that came from writing with one's left hand. I pointed that out and Mr. Langley smiled.

"Don't spit venom at me for saying so, Miss Porter, but I do believe you have a knack for this."

Quite the contrary, I found myself smiling at him. I thought that perhaps he was right for the first time and that in itself was a stunning realization. I had not ever been much good at anything outside of the world of book binding and to find that I had another talent gave me hope for my future. I may never bind another book or sell another volume but I had value outside of my family's trade and that was just as encouraging as it was depressing.

We arrived back at Mr. Langley's manor in no time at all. We had been discussing the case throughout the duration of the drive and continued our discussion as we entered the house and handed Bernard our hats and gloves.

"It's not emotional," I was saying as we entered. Mr. Langley was watching me with that look of thoughtful curiosity that commandeered his features whenever we were at work. "A suicide note should be emotional. I imagine it's the most emotional thing in the world, to decide to end your own life."

"But it does have a tone of resignation," Mr. Langley countered as we ventured into the dining room for luncheon. "I have heard of people who chose to commit suicide because they simply gave up. They had no fight left in them, no will to live. I imagine someone like that would appear quite emotionless."

I nodded in recognition of the point as the kind woman placed our lunch in front of us. I thanked her again, clasping her hand before she bustled off back into the kitchen this time. I looked down to the soup that she had brought out and felt my mouth watering at the delicious steam rolling off of it. I picked up my spoon and began to eat, considering Mr. Langley's argument. Apathy. Could that truly be reason enough to end your own life?

"He did not mention the method he chose to end his life. He does not mention the pills," I observed. Mr. Langley nodded.

"I noticed that as well. He hardly mentions the decision he has made at all. Outside of the brief, 'I have decided to kill myself' at the bottom, there is hardly no reference to his suicide at all, merely reasons for his dissatisfaction."

"He does not mention any friends or family."

"I thought that odd as well."

We continued in this way for some time, discussing our observations of the note and what they could mean. It was a riveting conversation that I became so mired in that I had not noticed that Miss Langley was not present until she entered through the front door which she did, as everything Miss Langley did, loudly and exuberantly.

"Oh Alexander, it's a lovely day," she exclaimed as she entered the dining room. She bent to kiss her brother on the cheek before settling in next to me at the table. She shot me a friendly smile just as her own lunch was set in front of her and I thanked the woman once more for her service. "I know that you enjoy this investigative work of yours but you must get out in the sunshine from time to time. You as well, Charlotte. Oh! I know! Why don't we all three go for a walk after lunch? Just a quick one."

"I'm afraid I have some business to attend to in my office but I am sure that Miss Porter would be glad for the fresh air," Mr. Langley answered, wiggling his eyebrows at me in jest. I smirked at him. He'd set me up.

"Oh yes!" Miss Langley shouted. "Just the two of us girls! I would love to get the chance to get to know you better, Charlotte."

"That would be lovely," I said as sweetly as I could manage, casting a glance in Mr. Langley's direction to ensure him that he hadn't gotten to me at all. In fact, I quite enjoyed Miss Langley's company and a walk outdoors and some fresh air was exactly what I needed after a night spent cooped up in a dusty old records room.

"I'll need Miss Porter returned to me in an hour. We have a lot of work to do tonight and there are a few matters we must attend to in preparation," Mr. Langley explained and Miss Langley and I nodded.

Having said his piece, Mr. Langley excused himself and marched off to his office to handle whatever business he anticipated completing within the hour. Miss Langley moved quickly and, forgetting most of her lunch, pushed me toward the door and waited while Bernard collected our hats and gloves. Then she looped her arm through mine and led me outside into the bright afternoon sun. I took a deep breath as we walked to the sidewalk, letting the air fill my lungs to their fullest. The air here was deliciously crisp, not at all the smoggy atmosphere of the middle class neighborhoods, the shops bordering the industrial districts. The rich could afford even cleaner air. The thought amused me and I smiled.

"I do hope Alexander isn't working you too hard," Miss Langley spoke suddenly and I looked over to see her kind smile aimed in my direction. I returned it politely.

"Oh no," I answered to ease her mind. "In fact, I find that I get just as lost in the work as he does. I find it all quite fascinating, you know."

"I find it morbid," she confessed. "Murder and lies, that's what my brother specializes in. I know that someone has to do it but I supposed I thought that was what the police were for. It's a dirty business that Alexander is involved in and, while I will always fully support any ambition he may have, I know there are quite a few among us who do not."

"Has Mr. Langley caused quite the scandal in the upper echelons?" I asked, a hint of amusement in my voice. Miss Langley heard it and smiled mischievously my way.

"No more than any other man his age," she answered with a roll of her eyes and we both laughed at that. She patted my arm as we turned toward the park. "Tell me, Charlotte, is there a man in your life?"

"Other than my father and my brother in law, I cannot say there is," I told her. "But I imagine you would have far more gentleman callers than I."

"Why's that?"

"You're beautiful with a dazzling wit and your family is among the wealthiest of the London elite. I imagine there are men clamoring for their chance with you."

"You would be surprised at just how many eligible young women my age there are. As for beauty, they have it as well. As for wealth, some have even more than I. And as for wit, well, not every man appreciates such a distinction. It seems there are far more eligible young women in London than men so, while my options are fairly limited, my brothers' knows no bounds."

I nodded. This fact did not surprise me. Mr. Langley was a very attractive man with his own means and a well-established family name. Not to mention his character. While most wealthy men did not value hard work and spent most of their days drinking with their friends or gambling their father's money away, Mr. Langley had taken on additional responsibilities and even ran his father's business. He seemed to have a sturdier head on his shoulders than most of the men that I had come into contact with. Though, I had to admit, that was not saying all that much. Still, women must practically throw themselves at him at the London social events. But I could not quite grasp why men would not react the same around Miss Langley. Then again, I never had understood the taste of men.

"Besides," Miss Langley said then, interrupting my thoughts as we entered the park. "You, my dear, have every single one of us beat in beauty and wit."

I gaped at her.

"It's true," she answered, nodding her head emphatically. "Those sparkling green eyes and those ringlet brown curls. And, to be frank Charlotte, I'm not certain how my brother gets through the day without staring at that ample cleavage of yours."

I felt my cheeks redden as I gasped. She laughed at that but then her laughter subsided when I did not join her.

"Have I offended you?" she asked, concerned.

"No," I answered honestly. "Just... surprised is all. I am not used to such blatant speech. I find it... refreshing."

She smiled at me and I found myself smiling back. I had spoken truthfully. I was always one to speak my mind but had lived a life of hiding that distinction from the parents and sisters who scolded me for it. Victoria especially. She should have been born a Lady or a Lady's maid. She knew how to be demure. She knew her manners, how to act around people deemed higher than us. She had always understood all of that as if it were ingrained in her very bones. I had always toed the line and struggled due to crossing it. My blunt speech and strong sense of righteousness had made me an undesirable in my own community but here, with these strangely open London elite, I was finding that the qualities that completely scandalized my sister and shamed my family were a novelty to them.

"Well, if there is one thing I am good at, Charlotte, it's honesty," she said and I chuckled.

"So tell me of the men you find interesting," I urged her and she broke out into an even wider smile.

"My mother has been pushing me to find my match as of late," she began. There was a bit of hesitation in her voice and she did not look at me when she talked but she continued all the same, though I imagine that was more because she needed to say it than I needed to hear it. "It's why I have been attending all of these events. I don't care much for many of them, you know, but one must be seen if one wishes to attract a mate. I've met many men who are interesting in their own way. Mr. Edwards likes to call upon me on Fridays. He sits in the drawing room and we have tea. But he is rather dull. He likes greatly to talk about politics and finds it intriguing that I enjoy the same but all of his opinions seem to come straight from the university textbooks and fall apart the moment they are questioned. Mr. Allen is interesting but only insomuch as he owns his own distillery and is never without an assortment of liquor. Mr. Foster is as handsome as they come but there is no depth there. Conversing with him is like speaking to a poodle."

I snorted at that.

"Is there no one that you are interested in?" I asked.

"I am interested in all of them," she said with a shrug and a roguish smirk. "But mostly for what they represent rather than who they are."

"What they represent?"

"Security, acceptance, privilege. When I marry, the pressure will be off of my shoulders. My mother will no longer keep tabs on my activities and society will no longer judge me for every year that I grow older and remain unwed."

I knew the feeling but I kept my comment to myself.

"Ideally, I would marry for love," she said quickly as if afraid that I had understood her to mean that marriage was no more than a business arrangement for her. "Of course, that would be the goal. But I have never been in love. I'm not sure that I would know what it felt like even if I was."

"I don't think it's exactly the feeling that you are expecting it to be," I said, more in thought than in conversation. She looked my way at that and urged me on. "I mean, I have never been in love either, not truly. But I have witnessed people who are. My parents, for instance, and my sister. I think it's like a feeling of completion, as if you are only half of a whole without them. I think it is simultaneously knowing they are the only one in this life who you want and that they are the only one who can infuriate you as they do. I think it's needing them as much as your next breath and knowing, as you know of air, that they will be there."

She smiled when I had finished.

"That's beautiful, Charlotte," she said.

"Thank you, Miss Langley."

"Please, call me Elena."

I smiled. "Elena."

"Well, I confess that I've never felt that way for Mr. Edwards, Mr. Allen, or Mr. Foster," she said with a huff and I laughed.

"Just the three of them hold your interest?"

"There are a few others. Mr. Cox and Mr. Morgan. Mr. Harrison..."

He was only one in a list but I found it peculiar that she should mention her brother's business partner at all. The others were a series of suitable gentlemen of notable families. Any parent would have been delighted for any one of them to show their interest in their daughter, much less all of them. But Mr. Harrison had been included in the prestigious list and I knew, for a fact, that the man was new money and had not yet earned a respectable reputation within the social circles that Miss Langley was in. His inclusion into the list posed some intriguing questions and I wondered if Mr. Langley was aware of just how high his sister's consideration of his business partner was.

I said very little else as Miss Langley delved into the details of the London social scene, describing the events she had attended and the women who I was likely to come into contact with during our upcoming theater outing. I could tell that there were quite a few of them that she did not particularly care for and I did not have to ask why. Miss Langley shared easily enough that she believed most of them to be uptight, snobby airheads and found it difficult to hold a conversation about anything other than fashion or gossip with any one of them. I nodded along, trying to keep the various names and dates in my head but it was proving an impossible task as the list seemed endless.

Finally, we had arrived back at the Langley's manor and we entered once Bernard opened the door for us, depositing our hats and gloves into his hands. Or rather, Miss Langley did. I was in the process of removing my gloves when Mr. Langley appeared and requested I did not as we were apparently about to leave again. So I slid them back on and waited for him to collect his own things. Once he did, we bid Miss Langley goodbye and made our way to the carriage.

"We will travel to your sister's home where you can tell her not to expect you until late this evening and then we will be going into town to pick up a few things for this evening," he told me and I nodded as I climbed into the carriage and we rode off at speed. It was quiet for a few moments before he asked me. "How was she?"

"Pardon?" I asked, looking up at him.

"Elena. I hope she didn't make you uncomfortable."

"She could never," I assured him with a smile. "She's very kind and quite friendly."

He nodded and smiled back. "That, she is."

Soon we had arrived at my sister's home. I told Mr. Langley that I would be quick and left him waiting in the carriage while I entered the shop. I would have invited him in but Victoria was stretched nearly to her limits lately and, after how I had left things between us this morning, I was not so certain that I wanted Mr. Langley's first impression of my sister to be her throwing me out of her family shop. Victoria was standing behind the counter. She glanced up from the meat she was wrapping as the bell chimed above the shop door. She looked surprised when she saw me but her surprise faded to suspicion when she saw the carriage waiting beyond the glass windows.

"I stopped by to tell you that I will be home late again tonight," I told her. "Some urgent business came up and Mr. Langley and I will be working on it rather late."

She raised a brow at me.

"Mr. Harrison will be working with us as well," I added, unsure of precisely why I did. I did not owe my sister an explanation, though it felt like I did. She watched me for a minute and then sighed.

"Very well," she told me. "Do try to be quieter this time though."

"I will," I promised, turning back and heading for the door. "Tell Liza not to wait up for me tonight,"

"Tell the birds not to chirp," Victoria answered and I smiled as I left the shop.

Mr. Langley stepped out of the carriage to help me back inside. I noticed he caught Victoria's eye and offered a friendly smile. She nodded in greeting but went on with her work the moment she had.

"I don't think she likes me," Mr. Langley said as he sat down opposite me in the carriage which had begun to move again.

"She doesn't trust you," I confessed. "But I wouldn't take that personally. She doesn't trust many people at all."

He nodded and turned his gaze to the window. He did not question my statement as most perhaps would. He just accepted it as though he understood the inclination to mistrust. Perhaps he did. We did not speak again until the carriage came to a stop and I emerged in front of an elegant dress shop in a part of town that I had never seen. I turned to look at Mr. Langley to find him smiling.

"Why are we here?" I asked.

"We are going to an auction tonight," he reminded me. "You'll have to blend in."

Then he pushed me gently forward and into the shop. It was a small boutique but the dresses on display were far richer than anything I had ever dreamed of wearing. The fabric itself would have cost me a month's wages at any other job I could have hoped to acquire. I resisted the urge to run my fingers over the smooth material as every head in the shop turned toward us. There were only three women in the shop. All of whom, it appeared, worked there. The oldest, though still perhaps only around thirty, moved toward us. She held her head high and pouted her lips as though consistently conscious of how they must appear.

"Can I help you?" she asked as she approached. Her gaze fixed neatly on Mr. Langley after an appraising glance my way which seemed to deem me unworthy of her attention.

"We need a dress made," he told her. "By this evening."

She did not seem surprised or put out by the suggestion though I knew how difficult of a request my employer had just made. She merely raised her chin higher and looked down her pointed nose at me.

"For her?" she asked as though I were not in the room.

"Yes, for her," he answered, a bit of irritation beginning to show in his tone.

"It can be done," she said. "For the right price."

"I don't-" I began but Mr. Langley stopped me, cutting off my claim that I did not have the money for such an undertaking with one of his own.

"I will pay it," he said.

"You will not," I argued, aghast at his suggestion. Mr. Langley paid me enough already. I would not allow him to buy me a dress of such quality as well. "I do not need a custom made dress. I can wear one off the rack."

The woman lifted the corner of her lip in a sneer and I fought the urge to smack it right off her pretty face.

"I expect our peers will know the difference," Mr. Langley said, nodding at the woman. "You will have the custom dress. Call it a business expense."

And with that, I was being pulled away from him and pushed to the dressing rooms in the back. My arguments fell on deaf ears as they led me away. Once we were in the back, just the four of us women, they pulled me promptly from my dress and measured every angle of my body, making comments with no concern that I could hear them and jotting notes down on a small pad. When they were finished, they dressed me again and gave me free rein to pick a fabric. I chose a deep purple satin that had an even deeper damask pattern ingrained upon it so that it was hardly visible at a distance. They snatched the sample from my hand and bustled off to get started on the dress. The woman from before handed me off to a waiting Mr. Langley as though I were no more than a child returning from day care.

"You may pick the dress up in two hours. Full payment is required now."

Mr. Langley moved to the counter to pay the dues and I moved, ruefully, to a nearby rack. I flipped through the beautiful gowns that I could not afford and thought, unhappily, about the one being purchased for me at that very moment. It wasn't that I was not thrilled by the prospect of a new dress. On the contrary, under any other circumstances, I would be absolutely elated and impatient to see how it turned out but I felt as though Mr. Langley had just purchased a gift for me and I had no way of returning the favor.

Once he had paid, he led me out onto the sidewalk.

"I would like to make payments to pay you back," I said the moment we were alone. He shook his head.

"I won't hear of it," he told me. "You would not have need of the dress if I weren't taking you to an auction for the elite. It is my affair and therefore I owe you the dress. It's a simple business transaction."

I shook my head at the lie but said nothing more on the subject. I had expected us to enter the carriage again but Mr. Langley walked off down the street instead. I followed after him and, once he realized my struggle to keep up, he slowed and extended an arm. I took it and grasped it as we walked, ignoring the whispers and glares of the passing young women on the street as best as I could.

"Mr. Harrison's office is just up this way," he explained as we walked. "I had hoped to stop in and see him. There are some matters of business we need to discuss and, seeing as you are also my business assistant, I would like for you to be present as well."

I nodded and walked on with him until we reached a small glass door with a name on it that indicated an office. Mr. Nathaniel Harrison, boasted the lettering on the door. Mr. Langley opened it and held it for me as I entered. The receptionist was a pretty young brunette who smiled up at us as we walked inside.

"Mr. Langley," she said with all the outright flirtation in the world in her voice. I resisted the urge to roll my eyes as her own slipped to me. "Miss...?"

"Porter," I introduced myself, smiling at her as I did. "Charlotte Porter."

"Ah Miss Porter, it is lovely to meet you. Are you a client of Nathaniel's as well?"

Nathaniel, was it? That was interesting.

"She is my assistant," Mr. Langley told her and the girl visibly relaxed. I could not help but smile though I did an excellent job at covering it with my hands while making a show of adjusting my gloves. "Is Mr. Harrison in? We have some things to discuss."

"In his office, Sir," she said, twirling a strand of her hair around her finger as she did. Mr. Langley simply nodded and pulled me along as he headed behind the front desk and toward the office beyond. He knocked once on the door before being invited in and entered as comfortably as one would his own home. Mr. Harrison burst into a grin when we entered. Mr. Langley pulled a chair out for me and waited for me to sit before he sat in the one at my side.

"Alexander," Mr. Harrison said in greeting. "Miss Porter. Always a pleasure. How's the investigation going?"

"Excellent. But that's not why we're here. My father wrote to me to inform me that he had instructed you to invest in an American cooperation on his behalf."

"Pelts," Mr. Harrison said with amusement as he sat back down at his desk. "Beaver pelts no less. He said he heard there was quite a bit of money to be made in the venture."

"He seems to be about fifty years off," Mr. Langley answered, matching the amusement in his friend's tone. "You did not send the money?"

"I remember our arrangement. I do not withdraw from the account unless the deal has been authorized by you."

Mr. Langley nodded. I noticed his shoulders slack a bit in relief.

"The senior Mr. Langley is a brilliant man," Mr. Harrison explained for my benefit, smiling at my obvious confusion. "But he is not quite up to date with the times."

I nodded in understanding, grateful for the explanation.

"Have you had time to reconcile the accounts of the American investments with the English ones?" Mr. Langley asked and Mr. Harrison nodded and just like that they were off on a discussion of business that I only moderately followed. They spoke rapidly and used terminology that they did not take the time to explain. After a few moments, I pulled a notepad and pen from my bag and began to take notes but they were speaking so fast that I only managed to compile a list of words that I would need to ask Mr. Langley to define later. I stared down at it in misery, mortified by all that I did not know, and hoped that Mr. Langley would not regret his decision to hire me.

When two hours had passed, my employer glanced at his watch and stood to shake Mr. Harrison's hand. Their business being completed, we left the office and headed back for the dress shop. I tried to ignore the glare that Mr. Harrison's receptionist shot me as we left but my efforts were in vain.

The dress was ready as promised and, when the woman asked me if I would like to wear it out, Mr. Langley answered for me that I would. So I followed the dressmaker to the back where they helped me into the gown. I gazed at myself in the mirror and could not help but smile. The dress was breathtaking, absolutely gorgeous. It accented every curve in a way that made them look utterly, naturally intoxicating. My cleavage, as Miss Langley would have been amused to see, was generous and my waist was cinched so that it looked smaller than usual. I appreciated that.

They placed the dress that I had worn in into a paper bag and I took it and exited the dressing room, rejoining Mr. Langley in the shop. His lips parted slightly when he saw me and his eyes bulged a bit. I tried to act as though I hadn't noticed his response as he cleared his throat and thanked the dressmaker but my reddened cheeks betrayed me.

"You look beautiful," he told me as we entered the carriage and I smiled courteously at him in gratitude.

We spoke of the business dealings on our way home. He allowed me time to ask my questions and I got many of them answered. He did not seem perturbed by my lack of knowledge but rather eager to share his own with someone who was genuinely interested. We were still speaking of the strange American economy when we entered his home to find that we were not alone. Our conversation halted abruptly, the words dying on my tongue, when I saw what awaited us.

In the drawing room directly on our right sat Miss Langley along with two older women and another of our own age whom I did not recognize.

"Alexander, you're home," Miss Langley said with a smile, standing to greet her brother. The other women stood as well. Mr. Langley entered the room and went to his sister, giving her a hug and a peck on the cheek.

"Elena," he said in greeting and then he turned to the middle aged woman next to her and gave her a hug as well. "Mother."

I felt my mouth drop open in surprise at the revelation. This woman was his mother. When I looked at her closer, I could see the similarities. She had the same striking blue eyes as her children, the same dark blonde hair though hers had begun to grey. She beamed at her son as though he lit up the room entirely on his own.

"Alexander," She breathed happily as only a proud mother could. She gestured to the women next to her. "This is Mrs. Abigail Walsh and her lovely daughter Felicity. Felicity is skilled at the pianoforte and I'm told has a lovely singing voice."

Felicity smiled at Mr. Langley and the awe in her eyes was nearly tangible. I bit my lip to keep from laughing at the obvious ploy. Miss Langley had told me that her mother was pushing her to marry. It seemed she was not the only child whose marital status concerned her. Mr. Langley smiled kindly at Felicity but backed away all the same.

"It is lovely to meet you both," he said and then, in a move that shocked us all, turned to me. He grasped me by the shoulders and pulled me into the room. Then he gestured toward me and announced. "This is Miss Charlotte Porter."

I waited for Mr. Langley to follow that introduction with my title or, at the very least, an explanation for my presence in his home but he did not and my hesitation forced an awkward silence. I glanced his way and was surprised to find him beaming at me, smiling broadly at my introduction.

"It's so nice to meet you all," I offered to break the tension. I noticed Miss Langley smirking behind her hand.

"It is lovely to meet you as well, Miss Porter," Mrs. Langley spoke first, having recovered from the shock much quicker than the rest of them, her manners and elegant grace returning to her more easily. She smiled kindly at me but I could see the suspicion in her eyes. I wished Mr. Langley would clarify my presence so that these women could see that I was no threat to them but he remained frustratingly silent on the matter and, as it would be rude for me to explain my occupation to them, so did I. Mrs. Langley moved on as effortlessly as she could. "I told Mrs. and Miss Walsh that you would be delighted to have dinner with them."

"Ordinarily, I would jump at the chance," Mr. Langley said kindly. "But I'm afraid I cannot tonight. Miss Porter and I have plans."

My gaze shot directly to him but he did not seem to notice.

"Plans?" his mother asked, eyes darting from her son to me.

"I'm afraid we are going out," he answeredBut do feel free to stay and dine with Elena. I know how she's missed you here in the city, mother. Mrs. and Miss Walsh, it was a pleasure to meet you. Please stop by whenever you wish. Miss Porter?"

He left me with no choice but to grasp his offered arm and follow him out of the drawing room, out of the house, and back into the carriage, feeling the skin on the back of my neck burning in the heat of their combined glares all the way.

8 An Auction

"Why would you say it like that?" I asked him once the carriage doors were closed behind us and I had settled into my seat as comfortably as I could in my uncomfortably tight bodice.

"Say what like what?" he asked so innocently I could slap him.

"You were very vague about the nature of our relationship. You led that poor girl to believe..." I trailed off, noticing that he was smirking at me. The realization dawned upon me in a gasp. "Mr. Langley! Have you just used me to get away from a potential suitor?"

He chuckled.

"You have to admit," he answered, leaning back in his seat. "The look on Miss Walsh's face was rather entertaining."

I hadn't the slightest idea how entertaining the look on Miss Walsh's face had been. I had been too concerned with the heat rising to my own. As it did now. I thought that perhaps I should be angry with Mr. Langley for having alluded to what he had alluded to with those women but, in truth, I could see the humor in it as well. So, despite years of breeding telling me that I should take offense and berate him for potentially dwindling both of our chances of attracting a mate, I could not hide my smile as I shook my head and gazed out of the carriage window.

"Why did you want to get away from Miss Walsh?" I asked after a moment and Mr. Langley looked up at me, seemingly surprised that we were still on the subject. "She seemed pleasant enough. Very pretty and, if your mother is to be believed, quite talented. Even I have heard of the Walsh family. They are a prominent family. As is your own. I imagine-"

"I do not care what her last name is," he said suddenly, the amusement in his voice entirely vanished. "I do not care that she can play the pianoforte or sing. I don't care that she has wealth or that she is highly sought after. None of that matters to me."

"It doesn't?" I failed to keep the surprise from my voice. He sighed.

"No."

"You have no interest in marrying?"

"I do," he answered, a wry smile spreading over his lips. "But not for status. And not to please my mother. I will marry whatever woman I choose."

He seemed so stern on the matter that I decided not to press him any further though I did find myself interested in this peculiar point of view coming from a man of his breeding. I decided, instead, to lighten the mood.

"I'm told the playing of the pianoforte is of vital importance in marriage," I joked and Mr. Langley's good-humored smile returned.

"Can you play the pianoforte, Miss Porter?" he asked, raising a brow. I laughed outright at that.

"I'm not certain I've ever been in the same room as a pianoforte, Mr. Langley. And I'm sure Miss Walsh and her ilk would run screaming from the room should I try to play one," I answered and he chuckled. "No, sir. I am rather far beneath the skills of pianoforte and singing."

He turned his gaze away from me to the surroundings passing us by through the window. The carriage fell silent and I do not believe he knew that I heard it when he muttered under his breath. "How could a woman like you be beneath anything?"

I fought to hide my blush the entire way to the auction and, once we had arrived, Mr. Langley and I emerged from our carriage into a throng of brilliantly dressed wealthy patrons making their way to the building directly ahead of us. We walked together, arm in arm, and entered the building from the street. It was a shop, I noticed as we entered, but perhaps the most elaborate one I had ever seen. The tall walls boasted paintings and sculptures for sale. There were strange knick knacks on the shelves all around us as well. The crowd moved straight through the shop floor, however, without even a glance back at the items. We followed along to a door in the back where each of our names were checked with a list before we were allowed in. We were stopped at the door but, once Mr. Langley explained that we were a friend of Mr. Dubois' and the guard got a good look at our ornate clothing, he nodded us past and I exhaled a breath in relief as we entered the room beyond.

It was infinitely larger than I had expected for the back room of a shop and it had been decorated with the lushest carpets and most elaborate wall trappings. Glasses of wine were available and many of the guests took one off of a tray being walked about by a servant. Mr. Langley passed on the alcohol so I did as well. Though I had always wondered what wine tasted like. We made our way to a corner and settled in for observation. After a few moments of scanning the crowd, Mr. Langley looked my way. I nodded and he offered his arm. I took it and we were moving through the crowd again.

"Good evening," a man said suddenly and we came to a halt. He smiled at us. "You must be new here. I'm quite certain I would remember seeing such a beautiful woman among us before."

I returned his smile as Mr. Langley extended a hand to shake the other man's.

He introduced himself. "Alexander Langley. This is my business assistant, Charlotte Porter."

The man nodded and smiled, though his eyes remained soundly on my breasts. I fought the urge to shift myself so that they were more covered, if that were indeed a possibility in this new dress. Mr. Langley followed the man's eyeline and, when he reached the destination, cleared his throat. The man blinked rapidly and then glanced back up at my employer's face.

"It is very nice to meet you both," the man said, though his gaze shifted back to me as he spoke and not to my face. "My name is William Peterson. This crowd could use some more youth in it. How did you find out about our little, er, gathering?"

"I am an acquaintance of Mr. Dubois," Mr. Langley said easily and the man beamed at him.

"Indeed?" Mr. Peterson queried enthusiastically. "Well, he is a very popular fellow around here. He contributes so greatly to the auction, both in buying and selling."

"Yes," Mr. Langley said. Mr. Peterson's gaze shifted back to my cleavage as he continued. "We had heard of Mr. Dubois' selling. I was under the impression that he sold quite a few of his friend Mr. Vincent Guillard's paintings not so long ago."

"Ah, yes, he did. After the tragedy. Poor man was so distraught, having to sell his dear friend's paintings. I imagine the money he made from the sale was some consolation."

Mr. Peterson's eyes sparkled when he spoke of profit but kept flitting back to me. Mr. Langley cleared his throat to regain the man's attention. It was louder this time, more impatient. I noticed that Mr. Langley's face was reddening. I had never seen Mr. Langley lose his temper before but I imagined that I was about to.

"Mr. Peterson," I said kindly and his eyes darted to my face. "Do you know if any of the paintings are still available? I do so enjoy Mr. Guillard's work."

"I'm afraid not, Miss Porter," he answered sadly. "They were all sold that day."

"Well, thank you Mr. Peterson," Mr. Langley said through gritted teeth. "It was nice to meet you."

His tone indicated that it was anything but nice to meet Mr. Peterson and he steered me away rather forcefully so that I was made to quicken my pace to keep up.

"Well," I said once we were out of earshot. "That was helpful."

"Was it?" he snapped.

"He was distracted enough to not realize how odd it was that we were asking so many questions about Guillard so I would qualify that as a success."

"I don't care for the idea of using you as a distraction, Miss Porter."

"He might know more about the paintings."

"We will find another man who does."

I opened my mouth to argue that there was no point in finding another man when this one seemed to have the information we were after but, after closer inspection of the fury on Mr. Langley's face, I thought it best not to argue. Though I did not entirely understand his temper, I knew that questioning it would only result in him turning his wrath upon me and that was not something I wanted to endure.

"Mr. Herbert," Mr. Langley said suddenly and I looked up to see Mr. Clyde Herbert standing in front of us, a glass of wine in his hand and a beautiful blonde woman on his arm. He smiled at us.

"Mr. Langley," he said kindly, though his eyes scrutinized every inch of us. "What a surprise. This is my wife, Mrs. Penelope Herbert."

"Mrs. Herbert," Mr. Langley greeted, kissing the offered hand as expected.

"Miss Porter," Mr. Herbert said in acknowledgement. "A pleasure as always. Have you talked Mr. Langley here into obtaining some art for himself? I know you have quite the eye for it."

"She is always bettering me in some way or another," Mr. Langley said with a smile. "This time, I suppose, she's making me more cultured."

Mr. and Mrs. Herbert laughed outright at that. I shot Mr. Langley a convincing smile right back.

"Oh, the two of you are the most adorable couple!" Mrs. Herbert gushed. Mr. Herbert awkwardly cleared his throat.

"No, dear," he corrected with a gentleness that I admired. "Miss Porter is Mr. Langley's business assistant."

"Oh," Mrs. Herbert said, her smile faltering. Her eyes roved over me once more in brand new appraisal and I could see the contempt in them. "I see."

"We were inspired by your Guillard, Mr. Herbert," Mr. Langley forged ahead as though he hadn't noticed the spite I had just incited. "I was hoping to purchase one for myself. Do you know if any are for sale tonight?"

"I'm afraid Mr. Dubois sold every last one the night that I bought mine," Mr. Herbert said with a frown. "But I have heard that some of the gentlemen who purchased one that night are seeking to sell theirs."

"Truly?"

Mr. Herbert leaned in closer and lowered his voice as he spoke. "Some of them no longer want them in their homes considering the... danger now surrounding them."

Mr. Langley nodded in understanding.

"Would you happen to know which of those men are looking to sell?" he asked.

"I do not," Mr. Herbert answered, straightening himself and returning to his normal voice. "But the treasurer keeps a record of every buyer. Perhaps he could tell you who else purchased Mr. Guillard's paintings that night."

"The treasurer," Mr. Langley repeated with a smile that I knew had more to do with the case than the prospect of purchasing artwork. "Thank you very much, Mr. Herbert. You have been most helpful. It was wonderful seeing you again. And you as well Mrs. Herbert."

Mr. Langley moved to walk away but Mrs. Herbert placed a hand on his arm and he stilled.

"Forgive me, Mr. Langley," she said sweetly. "but I am a mother, you know. My daughter is of an age with you and yet unwed. I would love to introduce the two of you. I think you may get along rather well."

I should not have been irritated by her solicitation. She was the mother of a wealthy young woman who had just met a handsome and wealthy young man. Of course, she would dutifully play the role of matchmaker. So I tried to gather my patience as I stood, looking out at the crowd to avoid watching the conversation taking place next to me. If Mr. Langley had not held my hand in the crook of his arm, I might have made an escape. Another servant was passing by at that moment with a fresh tray of wine glasses which looked all the more enticing now that I had been thoroughly scrutinized by half of the patrons here.

"Elizabeth, yes?" Mr. Langley asked and I could hear the joy in Mrs. Herbert's tone even without looking at her.

"Yes, you know her?"

"I know of her. My sister is Elena Langley. They are acquaintances, I believe."

"Oh, yes, Elena! We absolutely adore her!"

"She adores you as well."

I restrained my snort but could not contain my smile. I felt Mr. Langley's elbow make contact with my ribs and the laughter threatened to escape. But I bit my lip and waited.

"It was nice meeting you, Mrs. Herbert. You and your family are, of course, welcome to visit at any time," Mr. Langley said and then turned and guided me off back into the crowd. I know that the invitation was necessary and that he would be considered rude had he not offered but I also knew that Mrs. Herbert were likely to take him up on that and for some reason that bothered me. I could only hope that Mr. Herbert would come along as well as he seemed the only one of them capable of making interesting conversation.

The moment we started walking, our attention was drawn to a man who had stepped onto the stage. Mr. Langley glanced my way as everyone began to take their seats. We made our way to two chairs in the back and sat down.

"Good evening ladies and gentlemen," the man was saying. "I am the auction's treasurer, George Young, and I will be conducting the auction this evening."

Mr. Langley and I exchanged a glance. It was fortuitous that we had found out who the treasurer was so easily but quite unfortunate that he was conducting the auction. We would have to wait until the auction was over to speak with him. My eyes landed on the leather bound book in his arms. I thought that, perhaps, it might contain the ledgers. My estimate was proven correct when the first sculpture sold and Mr. Young took a moment to record the details in the book before speaking on the next item, a beautiful landscape painting.

"I should buy something," Mr. Langley said then, drawing my attention from the exquisite art. He was not looking at the painting, however, or at the auction at all. His gaze fell on a familiar dark haired man at the front. Mr. Dubois. I understood his intentions immediately. "Do you like this one?"

"Do I like it?" I asked, turning my attention back to the painting. "It is rather beautiful. And I imagine it would look lovely in your dining room."

"Thirty pounds," Mr. Langley shouted and all heads in the room turned to look at him. Mr. Dubois was among those that looked our way. He smiled in recognition when he saw us. Mr. Langley offered a polite wave in greeting and Mr. Dubois turned back around with the others. Mr. Langley spoke quietly to me. "That should go a long way in building trust. At least, now he has something on me. He knows I've illegally purchased a painting."

I nodded in understanding as the auction moved on. After what seemed like an eternity, the last item was sold and Mr. Young dismissed us all, inviting us to enjoy the rest of the wine and each other's company for as long as we liked. Everyone stood back up and most continued their conversations from before though a few left. The Herberts were among those leaving. Mr. Dubois was as well, though he stopped by briefly to say hello and to kiss my hand in that awkwardly drawn out way of his.

Mr. Langley tapped my arm and pointed to the treasurer. He was in the back of the room, ledger clutched to his chest as he spoke with one of the older gentlemen here.

"I don't believe he will allow two strangers to take a look at that ledger the way he's clutching onto it," Mr. Langley said. I eyed the man closely, formulating a plan of my own.

"If I could get him to set it down and distract him long enough, do you think you could locate the page and remove it?"

Mr. Langley's head snapped up in my direction and I saw the shock in his expression before it dissolved into a mischievous smile.

"Why, Miss Porter, I do believe I'm rubbing off on you and not in the best way."

I chuckled and extricated myself from him. Then I walked over to where Mr. Young stood with the older gentleman.

"Good evening gentlemen," I cooed as I approached. They both looked up at me, wide eyed. I smiled and leaned forward so that my bodice pulled tout. "I noticed you standing by the bar, Mr. Young. Is that because you're hiding all the good wine back here?"

His eyes had strayed to my chest but they shot back up to my eyes at my question.

"You have very discerning taste madam," he said with a smile. "I do happen to have a vintage or two I've been hoarding for myself. But perhaps I would be willing to share."

"I would so appreciate it if you would pour me a glass, Mr. Young," I said, batting my eyelashes like a fool. He grinned madly and moved behind the bar for a bottle and glass, setting down the ledger as he did. I caught sight of Mr. Langley moving our way out of my peripheral vision.

"Yes, well, I will speak with you later then, Mr. Young," the older gentleman said, giving me a look before he left. Mr. Young hadn't seemed to hear him. He emerged with a bottle and two glasses and walked to me as he poured them. He handed the full glass to me and I sniffed it delicately before taking a sip with him.

"Mmmm," I moaned as I sipped. Mr. Young choked on the wine in response to the sound and I saw Mr. Langley smirk as he flipped open the ledger. "Delicious."

"I am pleased that you like it," he said, raising a brow at my state. I waved the glass in front of me.

"Is this your shop?" I asked and he grinned.

"It is," he answered and I gasped.

"That is incredible!" I exclaimed. "My father has a shop of his own. Books. But it is nothing compared to this. This is quite impressive. All of this artwork you sell is so exquisite. I would love to hear more about where you find such amazing pieces."

He beamed proudly at the praise. Over his shoulder, I could see Mr. Langley flipping through the book. I stared daggers at the back of his head, willing him to hurry, as Mr. Young spoke.

"Many of them I find in my travels," he told me.

"Travels?" I widened my eyes and pouted out my lips. It worked. His gaze went directly to my mouth.

"Yes," he answered, clearing his throat. "There are so many undiscovered talents outside of London. I have been all over the world collecting these pieces. I would love to show you all of them."

His eyes remained on my lips and I imagined showing me artwork was not precisely what he had in mind. Mr. Langley moved and his knee hit the bar and Mr. Young started to turn at the sound but I stopped him with a hand at his collar before I knew what I was doing. He turned back to me, shocked and wide eyed at the sudden contact.

"I would love to hear of your travels," I said, stroking the side of his neck with a finger. It was far too bold but Mr. Young did not seem to mind. "I'm absolutely fascinated by men who travel."

He looked from my hand on his neck to my lips and something flashed in his eyes. It was a look that I was rather unfamiliar with, one that I was not so certain I had ever seen directed at me. Hunger?

"Miss Porter..."

"There you are, Miss Porter!" Mr. Langley exclaimed as he approached. "I've been looking all over for you. Mr. Young, a marvelous auction. Thank you very much for having us and thank you indeed for seeing my purchase safely loaded into my carriage. I do appreciate it. I'm afraid we must be going, though, it's quite late and it seems Miss Porter has had a bit too much to drink."

I faked a giggle as Mr. Langley took my arm and steered me away from the man. Mr. Young stared after us. When we had reached the door he called out. "You will return, won't you Mr. Langley? Miss Porter?"

"Of course!" Mr. Langley called back and then pushed me from the room. We walked swiftly through the shop and out onto the empty street. The moment our feet hit the pavement we both burst into laughter. "Brilliant job, Miss Porter. I have to say I'm quite impressed."

"Men are putty," I waved a hand and he chuckled.

"Perhaps we are," he agreed. "I was nearly too far distracted myself."

I brushed off the comment as the carriage rode up. I bid hello to the driver and climbed inside. It appeared that the painting was so large it took an entire seat on its own so Mr. Langley and I were forced to share the one side of the carriage. I slid onto the bench and waited for him to join. It was not a large seat and so we found ourselves quite pressed against one another. I tried very hard to ignore the strong, muscular thigh against my own as we settled in for the journey.

I felt my heart beating quicker in the silence. Perhaps it was the adrenaline from a night of covert investigation or perhaps it was my success at distraction, but I felt distinctly aware of our proximity in this small carriage. I breathed deeply to calm myself, scolding myself for being so affected by the nearness. I was certain that Mr. Langley was not experiencing the same reaction. But when I looked up at his face, I was stunned to find a heat in his eyes which matched my own.

9 Recompense

The driver hit a rough patch of road and the carriage bumped. Unintentionally, I slid right onto Mr. Langley's lap. His face was inches from mine, his expression a mask of some unreadable emotion. I felt my skin warming, my heart racing.

"Charlotte," his voice was a throaty whisper.

His utterance of my name shocked me back to reality. I cleared my throat, a bit too loudly in the crowded carriage, and jumped off of him, effectively hitting my head on the low ceiling above. I winced as I plopped, ungracefully, back into my seat. That strange expression was gone, that breathy whisper replaced entirely by a tone of concern.

"Are you alright?" he asked, moving forward to take a look at my head. I flinched away from him and he drew back as if I had stung him.

"I'm fine," I answered. "I- thank you. I'm quite alright."

He nodded but made no move to assist me though I could tell he wanted to. It was not in his nature to see a woman in need of help and not assist her. He opened his mouth to speak but thought better of it and looked away. Silence filled the carriage once more and I found my mind racing with the events that had just unfolded. Perhaps I had had too much wine. I had never had it before. Maybe it was stronger than the liquor I was used to. Maybe it affected my decision making faculties more than others. Or perhaps I was just a foolish girl caught up in the adrenaline of the evening and the attractiveness of my boss.

"I'm so sorry," I said then and his head snapped in my direction.

"Sorry?" he asked. The genuine confusion on his face would have made me laugh if I did not fear for my job.

"I didn't mean to- the carriage bumped and I-"

He smiled then and the action stunned me into silence.

"Were you worried that I thought you had intentionally sat on my lap?" he asked and I felt my cheeks grow hot. He chuckled. "It's quite alright, Miss Porter. I have witnessed your methods of flirtation, remember? I imagine if you truly intended to seduce me, I wouldn't stand a chance."

He winked to indicate the joke and I laughed along with him but there was confusion behind my laughter as well. Had I imagined that rippling current between us? Of course I had. Mr. Langley was a gentleman with a manor, a successful business, servants, and a dazzling family. I was a shop-girl with a gambling addicted father. And I would do well to remember that. The easy banter and comfort that I had been surprised to find with the Langley's would serve to make my employment in their household much more enjoyable but I had to remember that I was an employee. Nothing more. No matter how friendly this family was.

The carriage suddenly stopped and I saw the dark outline of my sister's house beyond. My face fell. I knew that she would be furious with me. I knew that it was well after midnight by now. I said goodnight to Mr. Langley as he helped me out of the carriage and made my way, as silently as possible, into the shop and up the stairs. But it did not matter how silent

I tried to be. Victoria was waiting for me at the top of the stairs with a clenched jaw, crossed arms, and a candle in hand.

I woke late the next morning and Victoria repeated the thrashing she had given me the night before for staying out late but this time it was for waking up late. I groaned at her admonishment and gulped down some breakfast before saying goodbye to Liza, Benjamin, and my father. Then I gave Victoria one final glare before I slammed the door behind me. Living with my eldest sister was going to kill me. Either that or this pounding headache.

By the time I made it to Mr. Langley's house, I was sure he would be ready to go and I was right. I moved from one carriage to another and tried not to wince as I sat down across from him, my head throbbing. The carriage began to move and we sat in silence for sometime. I had leaned back and closed my eyes but, when I opened them, I saw Mr. Langley smiling at me.

"May I help you?" I asked sourly.

"Please do not take this the wrong way, Miss Porter, but you look dreadful."

I snorted. "How could I possibly take offense to such kindness?"

He chuckled. I sighed.

"I'm afraid I did not get much sleep last night," I confessed. "After my sister spent the first hour of my arrival shouting at me for coming home late and waking the rest of the household, I might add, I had a rather restless night of sleep. But not to worry. I will simply rest my eyes for the journey and be good as new when we reach our destination."

He frowned then.

"This job has disturbed your family," he said and I could hear the guilt in his voice. It made me want to assuage his fears.

"My sister has disturbed my family," I told him. "I am an adult and must be trusted to come and go as I please. Though I know it is her house that I am living in. Still, I cannot neglect my duties."

I was aware that the sentence I had begun in an effort to make him feel less guilty had resulted in a rather unclear solution. Of course, the best possible resolution would be for Mr. Langley to stop requiring me at all hours of the night. But I did not blame him for it. It was the nature of the job. So I must find a way to work around it or find myself some new employment. My heart fell at the very prospect. I would have to speak with my sister this evening, explain to her how necessary this position was, not just for me, but for our family. She seemed to have forgotten what it was that had required me to seek employment in the first place.

"I think that, perhaps, your sister does not care for me," Mr. Langley said suddenly and I was drawn out of my thoughts to look at him.

"Which one?" I hedged. It drew a small smile from him.

"The elder."

"Ah. In all fairness, Victoria does not care for most people. Especially those who threaten the mundane routine of her life. Don't trouble yourself over it. In truth, I'm not so sure she cares much for me most days."

Another small smile but it was not enough. I could tell that he was troubled and I realized that there was a piece missing for him and his efforts to understand this puzzle. I sat up straighter in the seat and took a breath. I was not eager to tell him what I knew I must. I was mortified, in truth, at the absurdity of it.

"It does not help matters," I began. "That I did not tell Victoria the entire truth of my employment with you."

He raised his eyebrows in surprise but said nothing, his gaze urging me to go on.

"My sister is a very... traditional sort. She believes my time would be better spent finding a man to marry. But, if I am to work, she wants it to be in a position conventionally held by respectable women. Therefore, she believes me to be your receptionist. Nothing more."

I felt my cheeks warming at the admission. It was embarrassing to broach such a topic with my employer but he seemed genuinely concerned that my work had been affecting my family and I hoped that it would ease his mind to know that most of that tension had been caused by my own lie. To my surprise, he smiled.

"Receptionist," he repeated, settling back into his seat. "Not even assistant."

"I made the mistake of using that word the first time. She thought it was odd for you to give me such a title seeing as I'm..." I paused, sure I was about to do myself a disservice but wanting to be entirely truthful with him at the same time. "Not conventionally educated."

"Conventional education breeds only ignorance," He waved a hand in dismissal of my fears. "Well rounded, worldly knowledge is far superior."

I nodded, gazing down at my hands upon my lap, the feeling of mortification not yet subsided.

"What other employment does your sister find suitable to women?" he asked, a tone of curiosity in his voice. I glanced up at him.

"The usual, I suppose. We are part of the merchant's class and always have been. Many women we know assist their fathers in their shops until such time as they marry and then they assist their husbands. Victoria handles the customers at her husband's butcher shop. Outside of that, there are receptionists, governesses, companions-"

"Companions," Mr. Langley repeated, a smile upon his lips once more. "My sister is in need of a companion."

"She is?" I asked, stunned. I hadn't known that Mr. Langley had an open position for a companion for his sister. In truth, Elena Langley did not appear as though she needed to pay anyone to spend time with her at all. She seemed entirely capable of caring for herself.

"Absolutely," he answered. "Someone to help her navigate the London social scene as she is now eligible. I believe you would be just the woman for the job."

"Me?" I gasped in surprise.

"Of course, with the investigative work and the work of a companion, we would keep you quite busy. I imagine you would need to move into the house in order to be close to my sister should she have need of you," he said. His eyes were sparkling with the words he left unspoken. I would be close to assist him on his investigations without the suspicions or reprimands of my family. It was an interesting proposition and one which seemed to solve all of our problems. Victoria would find the role of companion to be an acceptable one, in fact one that I would be lucky to have found, and she would also be grateful for one less mouth to feed though I knew she would never tell me so. My absence would also make it easier for my family to secure a match for my younger sister without my spinster presence. And I would always be near for developments in our various investigations as well as to assist Miss Langley in one of the most exciting seasons of her life. It did seem to be the perfect solution and I could not deny the strain it would relieve for my family. Mr. Langley leaned forward. "I will need you near at all times, Miss Porter. You have become an asset to me."

"I believe you overstate my importance," I said to him and he shot me a smirk that made my knees weak in a way that made me glad I was seated. That was an issue. Perhaps living under the same roof as this man who seemed to have some sort of magnetic pull for me was not the best idea. Besides, the rumors would run rampant. Though I had never had much concern for gossip before. Still, I knew that would be a consideration in Victoria's mind as well. But the positives still seemed to far outweigh the negatives. "I will consider it."

That answer seemed to satisfy him and he nodded before turning his gaze to the carriage window. A few moments later, we had arrived at our destination, 142 Park Lane. Mr. Langley stepped out of the carriage first and held out a hand to help me down. Then we approached the house. The door was opened for us by a butler who then took us into the drawing room where we waited for the first man on Mr. Herbert's list. Randall Dabner was his name and, when he greeted us in the drawing room, he was precisely what I had envisioned. He was older with a round stomach that stretched nearly beyond the confines of his suit and white hair. He called for some tea and kindly invited us to sit which we did.

"Mr. Dabner," Mr. Langley began. "we are working with the police on a case of theft. A valuable painting was stolen from the London Museum of Art and it appears, through our investigation, that someone has been stealing paintings of the same artist from individual buyers as well. We are here because we have learned that you bought one of Mr. Vincent Guillard's paintings yourself. Is that true?"

"It is," he answered. "It is hanging in my study right now. A beautiful piece."

"Were you aware that someone was stealing that artist's works?"

"I was. Or at least, I had heard rumors. I had not believed them though."

"Why not?"

"Sounded like gossip to me. I don't place much stock in gossip, Mr. Langley."

Mr. Langley smiled.

"Nor do I," he told the man. "Though I'm afraid, in this line of work, gossip often means more than it seems. Have you noticed anyone loitering about your property lately?"

Mr. Dabner bristled at the inquiry.

"I imagine if I had, I would have notified the police as any sensible man would," he said with a sneer. Mr. Langley maintained his composed smile and rose to his feet. I did the same, placing my teacup and saucer on the table in front of us as I did.

"Of course you would," Mr. Langley agreed. "I am only here as a precaution. To warn you, if I may. It seems this thief is after the Guillard paintings and, if it is a collection he is hoping for, he will undoubtedly come for yours at some point. I would reevaluate your security if I were you, Mr. Dabner. Better safe than sorry."

Mr. Dabner frowned at that. He did not strike me as the sort of man who appreciated being told what to do within his own house. Though I imagined not many men did. Mr. Langley remained pleasant despite the glare he was receiving and bid Mr. Dabner good day before extending his arm for me to take and escorting me out of the house and back to the carriage. We had not gotten much from Mr. Dabner but I had not expected we would.

Undoubtedly, we would learn more from the men whose paintings had already been stolen but Mr. Langley was of the opinion that it was our responsibility to warn the others to heighten their security before we made inquiries into the thefts that had already occurred. He claimed that, if any of those on the list were robbed before he had the chance to warn them, he would feel guilty. Besides, there was always the chance that, if they were aware of the thief, they may even catch him for us and make our jobs far easier. So for the rest of the morning, we travelled to each man on the list and warned him of the danger. Most of them were kind enough, thanking us for the warning and sending us on our way, promising to cooperate with our investigation should they come into contact with any information they thought might help. A few were as cold and distant as Mr. Dabner and we were not well received but still, we got our point across and that was what mattered.

Close to midday, I found myself in the carriage with Mr. Langley under the assumption that we were returning to his home for lunch. I hadn't been paying attention to where we were, finding it nearly impossible to keep my eyes open after the late night and eventful morning. So when the carriage stopped and I stepped out to find myself in front of my brother-in-law's butcher shop, I could not hide my surprise.

"I think it best if you take the rest of the day to rest," Mr. Langley told me with a smile, helping me to the door. "I can see that you are exhausted and you will be of no use to me in such a state. We will return to our business in the morning. Here is your pay that I owe you for the last few days."

He handed me a small pouch and I took it. It felt much heavier than what I was owed.

"I kept you out late for two nights in a row, Miss Porter. There is a little extra in there for that," he said with a smile and then he headed back to his carriage but stopped, with one foot on the step, and turned back to me. "Do think on my offer, Miss Porter, I think it would benefit all parties."

I nodded in thanks and waved as the carriage took off down the road. Then I stared down at the pouch in my hands. The first payment for my father's debt. I would need to post it as soon as possible to avoid the wrath of those incorrigible thugs. With a yawn, I opened the door to the shop and entered to see both Benjamin and Victoria standing behind the counter. They had been speaking to one another but they stopped when I entered.

"You look terrible, Charlotte," Benjamin said with a smile. "Long night?"

Victoria elbowed him and he held his hands up in surrender. Despite my exhaustion, I smiled.

"In fact, it was. Mr. Langley has just given me the rest of the day off to rest," I told them as I approached the counter. Victoria raised a brow at me but, when I plopped the little pouch on the counter and the weight of it made a satisfying clank, her mouth dropped open a bit. "My wages for the overtime I've put in. So you can say whatever snide remarks you have to make about my coming home late but this is the result. It's enough for father's interest and to make a payment on the principle as well."

I folded my arms across my chest in satisfaction. I hadn't counted it but I knew, by the sheer weight of the pouch and Mr. Langley's unending generosity, that it would be more than what we needed for this week's payment. Victoria reached out and took the pouch, storing it safely behind the counter.

"I'm going to rest for a while and then I will take the payment to be posted," I told them. They exchanged a glance with one another.

"Perhaps you should wait until we close the shop, Charlotte," Benjamin said, warily. "From what your father has told us, his debtors do not seem to reside in the best area of London."

"Nonsense," I waved a hand, already making my way to the stairs. "I'd prefer to go in broad daylight if it's as bad as you say and if I waited for you to close the shop, it would be dark outside. I'll be fine on my own, Ben. I'll take a cab straight there and back."

He opened his mouth to argue once more but the shaking of my sister's head stopped him. They bid me a good rest instead and I thanked them and entered the residence. My father and younger sister were out. I assumed they were looking for employment for my father or a suitor for my sister or whichever of those things happened to cross their paths first. I was grateful for their absence as it allowed me to bed down in the living room for a quick and undisturbed nap.

A couple of hours later I awoke to remember that I had been too tired to eat. I found some leftovers in the pantry and ate a little before heading back down the stairs. I collected the pouch from my sister and bid them goodbye before opening the door and heading out into the street. It was easy enough to hail a hansom this time of day as most people were not about at this hour. I gave the driver the address that my sister had written on a small scrap of paper for me and he sped off to the destination. I pulled some of the coins from the pouch on my lap to pay the driver well in order to encourage him to wait for me.

Once we arrived, I did just that and asked him to wait. I would not be long. Then I turned back to the large but not well cared for gambling den ahead of me. I could hear the noise coming out of it even from the street. The rowdy sounds of riotous laughter and breaking bottles. I took a breath and steeled myself before entering. It was just as rowdy inside as it sounded from the street. Men were at tables all around, gambling and drinking, laughing and shouting. Many of them looked my way as I entered, apparently surprised by the appearance of a woman among them. I tried not to notice as I approached the counter directly ahead of me. A young man with a sharp nose and greasy hair narrowed his eyes at me.

"You lost?" he asked in a thick cockney accent.

"I am not," I answered as calmly as I could, trying to put what little forti-fication I felt into my nerves. "I am here to pay upon my father's debt."

The man nodded and pulled a thick ledger out from behind the counter.

"What's his name?"

"William Porter," I answered and he flipped open to the back and ran his fingers down the page. It seemed to take an eternity. The men around me were growing louder and louder. One of them had even shouted out at me, trying to get my attention. I kept my eyes on the man behind the desk, however, and he soon tired of the game.

"Here he is. Owes ten pounds this week,"

I placed the pouch on the counter and pushed it toward him.

"I would like for this to go toward his payment. It should be enough for the interest and for some of the principle as well."

He glanced from me to the pouch and back again.

"I'll need to speak with the boss before applying any payment over the minimum required," he told me. I nodded in understanding.

"Of course," I answered and he gestured for me to wait before ascending the stairs directly behind him to the second floor.

There was nothing for me to do but wait. I fidgeted with the ribbons on my bag for a few moments, trying not to look at any of the men around me, afraid of what they would say if they caught my eye. I heard bits and pieces of conversations here and there. I wasn't intentionally trying to eavesdrop but my mind sought occupation. A group of men nearest me were discussing plans to holiday at the coast. Some near the door argued over which brand of ale was the best. A man further into the room discussed a liaison with a woman he had had in such detail that it brought a blush to my cheeks. And then the two men in the corner were discussing a friend of theirs who had a painting of his stolen...

I froze, focusing in on their conversation. They were far away from me and difficult to hear at this distance. I found my feet sliding slightly toward them before I was consciously aware of the action.

"Bought it from one of those illegal auctions, you know," the first man was saying, lowering his voice so that I had to strain to hear him. "Then it gets stolen only weeks later. Strangest thing. Harry has an original Rembrandt in his foyer. Why the thief would take a Guillard over that, I haven't the slightest clue."

"Especially now," the other man told him. "That the value is nowhere near as high as it was right after that man committed suicide. If I were going to steal a man's paintings, that would have been the right time to do it. Now that's passed and everyone knows they're stolen, I doubt he will make much of a profit off of them."

"If he can even sell them at all. I heard..."

But I wasn't listening anymore. My heart was thrumming in my chest at the realization I had just had. Greasy hair was returning to the desk but my mind was elsewhere.

"Your payment has been posted, Miss Porter. We will see you in a week for the next one."

I thanked him and left the establishment but, when I returned to my hansom, I told the driver not to take me home. I had a new destination in mind.

10 Theory

To say that Mr. Langley was surprised to see me standing in his drawing room would be an understatement. Bernard had let me in and had gone straight to Mr. Langley to tell him of my arrival. He must have taken the news to mean that something was wrong for he came bolting down the stairs and into the living room like a madman fleeing the scene of a crime. The irony was not lost on me as he ran a hand through his tousled curls to smooth them out and looked me over, wide eyed, to see if I was harmed.

"Miss Porter, I- forgive me, are you alright?" he asked. I found it rather amusing to see him so out of sorts and could not contain my smile. He smiled back, shoulders relaxing as he realized I was unharmed and rather amused by his concern. I was touched as well, if I were being honest, but I would not allow that to show.

"I am fine, Mr. Langley," I assured him. "I apologize for disturbing you in your home."

"You could never be a disturbance. Would you like some tea?"

"That would be lovely."

He nodded to Bernard who went off to retrieve the tea and then gestured for me to sit. I did and he took up a position next to me. I was watching the place where Bernard had vanished down the hall to fetch the tea, undoubtedly from that kind woman who served us our meals.

"What is the name of your cook?" I asked absentmindedly.

"What?" Mr. Langley responded in surprise.

"The woman who always brings us our meals, cooks them, and makes our tea. What is her name?"

"Maggie," he said, smiling and shaking his head. "I do hope that isn't the reason you've driven all the way here this afternoon."

I laughed outright at that. "No. I had intended to ask long before now. I just hadn't gotten around to it."

Just then, Bernard entered the room once more, this time with a tray of tea and things for us to nibble on as we sipped. Mr. Langley thanked him and set out my tea for me, offering me a sweet as he did. I declined at first but then he urged me to partake and so I relented and bit into the offered pastry, feeling the strange sweet flakes disintegrate upon my tongue in a way I had never before experienced.

"Now, what brings you here? I thought I gave you the rest of the day off."

"You did. And again, I apologize for the intrusion, but I overheard something this afternoon which got me thinking. You see, we noticed before how odd it was that the thief might steal a Guillard with a Monet so close by. We've been keeping an eye on the auction and the methods of resale but what if the thief is not interested in selling the paintings?"

Mr. Langley blinked at me, thoughtful.

"The men I overheard speaking of the theft this afternoon were saying how foolish it was of the thief to steal the art after their value had dwindled. After Mr. Guillard's suicide, the value of his artwork soared and Mr. Dubois, his friend, was able to sell them off at a high profit. If the thief were stealing the paintings in an effort to resell them, he would have stolen them then. So why wait all these weeks before beginning to steal them?"

"Why, indeed?" Mr. Langley asked, stroking his chin.

"I think there is something personal about these paintings, something specific to Vincent Guillard. Do you remember the encyclopedia?"

"The hollowed out book which housed a stolen pocket watch that you sussed out in a matter of seconds?" Mr. Langley asked, eyebrow quirked and a smile on his lips. "I do."

"I have heard of people hiding things in the bindings of paintings as well. A man whom my father was friends with, a reseller of art, told us that people had come to him before and asked him to hide things for them in the bindings of the paintings. Money, wills, important documents. They wanted to hide it somewhere that thieves would not expect rather than putting it in their safes which would be the first place a thief would check."

Mr. Langley nodded, thinking.

"So you believe someone may have hidden something in one of Guillard's paintings," Mr. Langley said slowly. "But then why would they be attempting to steal all of the paintings? Wouldn't they only need the one?"

"Perhaps they have forgotten which one," I said. "Some of Guillard's paintings were old. If I were going to hide something of value in the binding of a painting, I would choose a painting that was not high in value itself so as not to attract attention and I likely wouldn't care much for the painting if I were to allow it to be desecrated in such a way so I may not remember precisely what it looked like. Most of Guillard's paintings seem to be of the park and all of them very similar."

"So why not come out with it and tell the art community that they are looking for something important bound behind one of the paintings?"

"Perhaps they are concerned whoever finds it will keep it for themselves or perhaps they are too embarrassed to admit such an oversight."

Mr. Langley considered for a moment and then smiled.

"It's a good theory, Miss Porter, a very good theory," he praised and I could not help but smile. "Brilliant, in fact. But I'm curious. Where were you that you overheard two gentlemen speaking of the paintings? We tried all morning to get men to talk about the thefts."

I cleared my throat and looked away from him then, staring down at my hands fidgeting in my lap. I knew that I could tell him this and trust him not to tell anyone else. I wasn't sure how I knew that, having only known this man for a few days myself. But somehow I knew that he would understand and I didn't see the point in keeping secrets from him. In fact, I did not want to keep secrets from him. And I felt that, if I were to move into his home, though I had not yet decided whether I would or not, it would not be fair to settle myself into his house with such secrets between us. I took a breath and then looked up into his eyes which I found already gazing into my own.

"I took a hansom to the East End this afternoon," I said and I saw the crease in Mr. Langley's forehead as indication that he knew as well as I what a terrible area that was. Still, I forged on. "I had to make a payment, you see. My father... he owes money to the wrong sort of people. Gambling. I had to make a payment to them or..."

I felt tears welling up in my eyes. How ridiculous. I had never cried over this before. And I wouldn't now. I straightened my back and wiped the back of my hand over my eyes. Then blinked a few times to stop the tears.

"Well," I said, firmer this time. "It was there that I overheard the men talking."

"Oh, Miss Porter," Mr. Langley said, placing his hand upon my own. The intimate touch sent a shiver through my spine but the effect was diminished somewhat by the tone of pity in his voice. I pulled my hand away.

"I don't wish to speak of it," I told him then, my mind made up. "It is of no concern to you, Mr. Langley."

"Miss Porter, if I can help, I would like-"

"Please," I stopped him. "I've had my rest. I am ready to resume my work. If you have no business to take care of this afternoon, it may be prudent to visit the homes of the men whose paintings were, indeed, stolen."

Mr. Langley nodded, though the pity remained in his eyes, and fetched his hat and gloves from Bernard. In a matter of moments, we were on the road again, back to our list but this time of the ones that Mr. Herbert had circled as knowing those men had had their paintings stolen as well. Mr. Langley said nothing more about my afternoon errand and chose, instead, to prattle on about the case and his potential theories along the way. I welcomed the distraction and admired the way in which he threw himself into his work.

We arrived at each house in turn and interviewed the men to very little avail. Each of them described the scene as similar to what we had witnessed at the London Museum of Art. The Guillard painting had been stolen but nothing else. All of their remaining valuables, some of which were much more valuable than the painting, remained perfectly in tact. None of the men had the slightest indication of who could have stolen the painting. None of them had seen anyone loitering outside of their homes to learn their movements. None of them had noticed anything out of the ordinary in the days leading up to the theft at all. I was beginning to feel hopeless by the time we arrived at the home of the last victim on the list.

I was feeling disappointed in our search as Mr. Langley and I were let into the grand foyer by the butler who turned to fetch his master but got no farther. The man we had come to see, Mr. Adams, was walking into the foyer alongside none other than Mr. Louis Dubois. Mr. Langley halted the moment we saw him and I could see the narrowing of his eyes in concentration. Mr. Adams and Mr. Dubois had been conversing genially but they stopped speaking when they saw us, though the pleasant smiles remained on their faces.

"Mr. Langley," Mr. Dubois said kindly. "Miss Porter, a pleasure to see you again."

"And you as well, Mr. Dubois," Mr. Langley answered with a smile of his own.

"Mr. Adams and I were just speaking of the auction last night," Mr. Dubois said, his eyes sparkling with enthusiasm. "That painting you purchased was exquisite, Mr. Langley."

"Thank you. I am never disappointed in the finery I obtain when I allow Miss Porter to dictate my purchases. She is far more versed in art than I am."

"Indeed?" Mr. Adams asked then, his eyes turning to me and roving over me in appraisal. "Perhaps she should accompany me to the next auction then. Instead of my dimwit sister. She had me bidding on an Anderson, can you believe it?"

"Who is Anderson?" Mr. Langley asked.

"My point precisely!" Mr. Adams exclaimed, throwing his hands into the air. Mr. Dubois burst into laughter and Mr. Langley chuckled kindly along. I smiled but I found myself feeling unable to laugh at a man referring to his sister as a dimwit. It seemed cruel.

"I hope we haven't intruded on your company," Mr. Langley said then.

"Not at all, my dear man. Louis wrote to me last week asking me to stop by to admire my Guillard."

"Indeed?" Mr. Langley asked. "I thought your Guillard painting had been stolen, Mr. Adams."

"The one in the drawing room, yes," Mr. Adams said, a triumphant smile on his face as he continued. "But they didn't get the one in my study."

"You had two? And you've come to see the one that remains?" Mr. Langley asked, his interest piqued as he turned to Mr. Dubois. There was a brief moment of hesitation before Mr. Dubois' smile turned sad and he waved a hand.

"Sometimes I regret selling the collection," he confessed. "I miss my dear friend so greatly. It helps with the grieving to visit his work from time to time. Though I am glad that they are being thoroughly enjoyed."

"You visit all of his paintings?" Mr. Langley asked.

"No of course not. Only those which ended up in homes of dear friends and only when I am already due for a visit. Mr. Adams, it is always a pleasure to see you. Please, don't hesitate to stop in at any time."

"Of course, Louis, and you as well."

Mr. Dubois headed past us for the door but Mr. Langley was not finished with his questions. He called out after him. "Pardon me for asking, Mr.

Dubois, but, as Mr. Guillard was such a close friend of yours, do you not have any of his paintings in your own home?"

"Of course, I do," he answered, still smiling. "But only a few. I did not feel right about hoarding such talent from the world."

"Where are they displayed? I did not see them when we came to visit. I would think a man who wanted such artwork displayed would have hung it in his foyer or his drawing room where he receives the most visitors? There were many other such works there but I did not notice a Guillard."

At last, I understood what Mr. Langley was alluding to. If Mr. Dubois was the friend that everyone said he was to Mr. Guillard, he would have proudly hung his friend's paintings in his home for the world to see. That is, unless he was somehow bothered by his association to such a man. Or if he had torn the paintings apart to find something within their binding. I felt my own arm tighten around Mr. Langley's but if he noticed he gave no indication. Mr. Dubois was smiling still but his eyes had gone cold.

"Very well, Mr. Langley," he said, the pleasantry still there but there was an underlying tone of anger in his voice. "You've discovered my secret. You must understand how painful it is for me to be reminded of Vincent in my own home. I took the paintings down. I could not bear the grief they brought me whenever I entered my own foyer."

"And yet you've come here to gaze upon one again," Mr. Langley said.

"Grief in small doses is healthy," Mr. Dubois said, his jovial attitude back. "Helps one to heal."

"That it does," Mr. Adams spoke up from behind us. "Good day, Louis. I will see you at the next auction."

"Good day, Mr. Adams, Mr. Langley, Miss Porter."

With that, Mr. Dubois took his leave. Mr. Langley watched him go before turning back to Mr. Adams and giving him the same warning we had given the others. To heighten his security and lock up his remaining painting. Then we left, entering our carriage once more. Mr. Langley seemed thoughtful as we walked to the coach and did not say a word until I had stepped onto the first step.

"Could you look behind a binding?" he asked, brows creased in thought as he did. "Without damaging the painting?"

"My skill is in book binding," I answered. "The binding of a painting is different but I believe I could. If I had the correct equipment."

"Would such equipment be at your father's shop?"

"It would but—"

"Excellent," Mr. Langley interrupted and was off giving the driver instructions before I could protest. He rejoined me a moment later and, before I could speak, continued. "We will go to your father's shop and collect the equipment you need. I hope he does not mind our borrowing it for the evening. We can return to my house and you can practice on that painting we bought at the auction. If you are successful, we may be able to talk some of the men on our list into allowing us to look behind the bindings for anything out of the ordinary. If they knew that the painting would not be harmed, they might be more inclined to allow us to investigate. In fact..."

He spoke on and on about his new plan to search the bindings of each painting one by one. I made no further attempts to interject. In fact, I was not sure how to tell him that there was no shop to go to, no equipment to borrow. I had told Mr. Langley just this afternoon of my father's gambling debts. It was quite a leap to go from owing debt to seeing the consequences of not paying said debt. I was not so sure I was ready for that conversation. Nor was I sure that I was ready to see the ruins again myself. It had been a few days since I last saw the remnants of my father's shop, the smoldering rubble that had been our livelihood. I was not so sure I was ready to face it. I wanted to tell Mr. Langley that. Truly, I did. I wanted to tell him he was wasting his time and to call to the driver to reverse course but I did not know how to tell him and I wasn't sure I would have been able to even if I had.

So when the carriage came to a stop and I realized what we were about to step out into, I panicked and threw myself in front of the exit. Mr. Langley's eyebrows creased in confusion.

"Miss Porter?" he asked.

I opened my mouth to say something, anything. To explain what he was about to see, to prepare him, but the words would not come. All I could say was. "Please don't be angry."

And then I was stepping from the carriage without his assistance. I did not want him to touch me. I felt soiled in a way, having not told him to turn the carriage around, having not stopped him, knowing that I was wasting his time. He followed me out, eyeing me in curiosity all the while. When he stepped fully out of the carriage and his eyes took in the sight awaiting him, his mouth fell open. I had my eyes closed, tears already sliding down my cheeks, but I forced them open. I forced myself to look at the shop that I had been avoiding. My entire childhood, everything I had ever known, my family's livelihood burned to ash in front of me.

It was no longer smoldering, the fire having long gone out. The ground was covered in soot and ash. Most of the rubble had been pushed back away from the street. I saw the shop sign at the front. Only half burned away, it read Port- Booksh-. I closed my eyes and felt the tears on my cheeks. I buried my face in my hands and tried to picture it as it was before. Porter's Bookshelf. The red-paned windows, the displays of elaborately decorated tomes, the leather bindings and the smell of the printing press. The noise it made that would be a ruckus to anyone else but lulled me to sleep at night.

I felt a strong arm around my shoulder. Then another. And Mr. Langley was pulling me into him in an embrace. I knew it was not appropriate. I knew that he was my boss and I was his employee. I knew that there were likely neighbors watching because we were standing in the middle of a busy street. But I didn't care. I needed the comfort. I needed the security. So I turned into him and wiped my tears on my gloves. We stayed like that for some time. Mr. Langley did not push me away. He did not even speak. He seemed to know that I needed some time and so he gave it to me.

When I had pulled myself together, I extricated myself from him and looked up to find him watching me.

"Why didn't you tell me?" he asked then. It was spoken as a whisper but there were more emotions than I could name in his tone. At the forefront, however, was anger. I was surprised by it.

"I beg your pardon?" I asked, blinking at him.

"Miss Porter, I am a private investigator. Did you not consider that perhaps I could assist you in finding who did this to you?"

"What do you mean? I never said it was arson."

"There is a smashed lantern on the edge of that rubble," he said, raising an eyebrow. Of course he had noticed that.

"I can't afford to hire you," I said. I saw a flash of fresh anger in his eyes at that and he clenched his jaw.

"You think I would have charged you?"

"You wouldn't?" I gaped at him. He clenched his fists and turned away from me. He ran a hand through his hair and took a few steps before turning back to me. His anger had subsided somewhat but it still had me stunned, frozen in place.

"Of course not," he said then, his voice calmed slightly. He took a deep, steadying breath, casting his eyes out at the burned rubble once more, before turning back to the carriage. He placed a hand upon my shoulder and led me gently back to the coach, helping me back inside. Then he told the driver to take us to my brother-in-law's butcher shop.

We said very little to one another on the ride back. I stared out the window, trying to keep my tears at bay. It was difficult seeing my father's shop, or what little remained of it, and it had affected me more than I had thought it would. Mr. Langley must have known what I was doing for it was too dark outside for me to be as invested in my surroundings as I appeared. That was another thing. It was dark which meant it was late. Not as late as I had returned the two previous nights but late enough, I'm sure, for Victoria to have something to say about it.

I was right, as it turned out, and my sister began in on me the moment I arrived. Everyone was still awake and sitting in the living room. Victoria did not seem to mind admonishing me in front of all of them. Perhaps it was my exhaustion for having not slept enough the past few days, perhaps it was that my emotions were raw and my nerves were frayed from the afternoon's events, but I did not feel too much like putting up with it tonight.

"You cannot be coming home at all hours of the night, Charlotte!" Victoria was shouting at me for the tenth time in two days. "Mrs. Haverford saw you returning last night and came into the shop to inquire after your well being! Do you have any idea how mortified I was to-"

"Mrs. Haverford can mind her own business and you can too!" I exploded. It was the first time I had ever said anything in response to my sister's tirades. It drew the attention of the entire family. My father set down his newspaper, Liza set down her sewing. Even Benjamin opened his eyes from his dozing to look our way. Victoria's eyes widened and her face grew even redder.

"It is my business, Charlotte!" she shouted back. "This is my house! This is my family! And I don't appreciate the sort of gossip you are inviting to my door! You know, as well as anyone, what gossip can do to a shopowner's reputation and therefore business! I will not have you threatening my family's livelihood!"

"You care far too much about what those shriveled up old women say about you in their teacups, Victoria! You always have!"

"A reputation is all a woman has in this world, Charlotte! You never understood that! You've always been so... difficult! Always! Perhaps that's why your fiancé found a woman who was not!"

I felt my lips part in shock. The silence in the room was palpable. The only noise was Liza's small gasp. Benjamin had risen to his feet now but remained where he was, unsure of how best to interfere. For the umpteenth time today, I felt tears welling up in my eyes. I clenched my jaw, released a breath, and turned on my heel. I stomped into the bedroom that had become my father's and, grabbing a small bag, I began shoving what little of my belongings I had into it.

"Charlotte," Victoria said, more calmly now, her anger having been expelled. "Charlotte, please. What are you doing?"

I set the bag on the floor next to Liza as I packed it. My younger sister gazed up at me wide eyed.

"You won't have to worry about it anymore, Victoria," I told her, tears streaming down my cheeks. "I'm terribly sorry to have been such a nuisance to you."

"Where are you going to go?" she asked, exasperated.

"Mr. Langley has offered me the post of his sister's companion. Paired with my job as his receptionist, I will have to be near his family night and day. He has offered me lodgings in his home, just next to his sister's room. I've just decided I'm accepting it."

Victoria's mouth dropped open at that. She wasn't the only one. Liza's eyes only grew larger.

"Charlotte," Benjamin said, stepping forward for the first time. But his usually calming presence did nothing to lessen my anger, nor my determination to be away from my sister. "Please, be rational. Think calmly about this. There are already rumors circulating about your involvement with that man. Do you really want to fuel that fire?"

"Gossip, again!" I exclaimed, throwing my hands in the air as a wicked laugh escaped me. "When are you going to realize that I do not care what those women are saying about me? I don't care about rumors. I don't care about gossip. I'm already twenty five years old. Unmarriable by London standards. So what does it matter if my reputation is ruined? I couldn't find a husband when it was not. I won't find one if it is."

The truth in the statement shocked the room into silence. Still seething, I gathered my bag and headed for the door but Benjamin stood in my way.

"Charlotte, if this is your decision, then we will support you," he began. Victoria made a sound but he silenced her with a glare over my shoulder before continuing. "But stay here tonight. Think it over. There's no sense in showing up at that man's house this late anyway."

I hardly heard him. Bag slung over my shoulder, I was already making my way toward the door, chin held high in the air and jaw tensed in my fury. Benjamin called out once more behind me as I wrenched the door open and fled down the stairs to the shop but I didn't even pause to listen. My feet hit the pavement outside a moment later as I hurried on to the corner to hail a hansom. It was late, very late, and, despite my glancing furiously back and forth for what must have been at least ten minutes, no hansoms were coming. The street was desolate, silent. Not a soul was about this late at night. None but mine. And whatever London ghosts roamed these streets at this hour. I peered into the window across the street, narrowing my gaze absurdly. The chances of Mrs. Haverford watching me from out of her windows this late at night were miniscule but, if she were, I wanted her to know that I was watching her right back. I hoped it, at least, gave her a fright.

Giving up on my search for a carriage, I marched on across the street, resigned to walk the entire way to the Langley Manor myself. The moment I stepped out into the road, my shoe sunk into a particularly wet bit of London street sludge and I sighed as I extricated it and walked on. I could not seem to catch a break. Victoria, apparently, found it impossible to understand the importance of what I was doing, likely because she didn't know the truth of it, despite the fact that I had been practically single handedly paying the interest on our father's loans while her and Benjamin's income went to maintaining the shop and providing for our father and sister. She worried so greatly about what those thugs might do if our payments ceased and yet was determined to admonish me every time I came home late from the job which was making those payments possible.

I rolled my eyes and hoisted my bag further up my shoulder. Granted, I could be more respectful of the members of my family whom I was now living with and try harder not to wake them up at such an ungodly hour. Well, that was why I was taking Mr. Langley up on his offer.

Right?

My feet slowed. My righteous indignation waned. Was I subconsciously grasping onto any excuse I could find to spend more time with this man? I enjoyed the time we spent together as it was, even though I was merely in his employ, and I had begun to lose track of time whenever we were together. I had never done that before. Not even when I was engaged. No. I shook my head but I stopped walking all the same. That's when I heard it. The abrupt halt in stride of another. A soft intake of breath.

The hairs on the back of my neck stood on end, the rhythm of my heart ticked steadily upward. I craned my neck slightly to the side and heard the quiet shuffle of feet from the pavement. My eyes went wide but I snapped my head back in a forward direction, trying my hardest to appear normal despite every nerve in my body screaming in warning. I had a decision to make and one which required an expedient resolution. Someone was following me. For what purpose, I could not be sure. But I needed to get somewhere safe, somewhere inside, and quickly. Mr. Langley's house was too far away and besides, I wasn't so sure anymore that it was the destination I desired. I did not know anyone in this quarter of London. My only hope was to head home, as quickly as I could, taking the streets that were the most well lit and praying I could scream loud enough for someone to hear if it should come to that. So, without pausing a moment more to think about what I was doing, I hurried across the street to the other side and headed back toward my sister's shop.

If my pursuer had walked ahead to follow me across the street, I did not pass him. I had hoped he believed himself to be caught and had moved on but I knew in my gut he was likely waiting in some shadow until he could emerge to follow me at length once more. Sure enough, my suspicions were realized when, a block away, my anxious ears heard the soft padding of his footsteps at least ten feet behind me.

My hands were shaking so I hid them in the folds of my dress. What had I been thinking? Running out onto the dark London streets in a rage, carrying all of my personal belongings on my back, when I was perhaps more aware of the dangers of doing so than any other woman in the city. I whispered a silent curse. What was this employment doing to my sanity?

I turned a familiar corner. He followed. I hastened my pace, I couldn't help it. My heart was hammering against my chest and my breaths were coming in quick and shallow gasps. Who was this man? What did he want? Was he just some common criminal? Was he one of the thugs who had threatened my father and burned my family's livelihood to the ground? Was it someone connected to the case that Mr. Langley and I had been investigating? Could it be the infamous art thief out to halt the progress we had been investigating in the case? And how long had he been watching me? How long had he been following me? To know I would be outdoors at this late hour on these empty city streets? To see that I had left the shop? Shivers shot through my spine and I picked up my pace once more. I was practically running now but the shop was in sight, the light still on as if either Benjamin or Victoria hadn't believed I would actually leave. I made a mental note to be upset about the insult later. For now, I was singing their praises.

I made it to the door just in time, wrenched it open and fled inside. My bag hit the floor with a thud as I bolted every lock the door had and leaned my back against it, panting and shaking. As I fought to catch my breath, to calm my shaking nerves, I saw the shadow. He passed by the window directly to my right, the one which usually boasted of the sales of the day. The shadow of a man, tall but not overly muscular with a bowler hat and the collar of his top coat popped up, passed over the long butcher's counter in the lobby before disappearing into the night as quickly as he had come.

I blinked once. Twice. Trying to clear my head, trying to gather my wits. Then, dully and almost without thinking, I bent to gather my things and made my way back up the staircase to the apartment above. I would sleep here tonight, in the living room with Liza as I had before, and I would never venture into the dark London streets alone again. Or rather, I would lay next to Liza staring into the darkness because I was highly doubtful sleep would come to me now.

11 The Frenchman

Despite the nerve wracking events of the previous evening, I had quite a bit of time to consider my options for residence as I lied awake, praying my heartbeat would return to normal and wondering, honestly, if it ever would. I realized then that there was a matter which I had not taken into consideration in my fury and sudden decision. Elena. The position of her companion had been offered to me. A chance to earn even more money to pay upon my father's debts in hopes to rid ourselves of them quicker. How could I turn such a post down? And it was expected that a wealthy woman's companion, especially an unmarried one's, would live within her household with her. In fact, it would be considered odd had I not. So, if I wished to take on the additional responsibilities of the new position, it would be imperative that I took up residence in the Langley manor. And I rather though I did want to assume that post.

The next morning, given the time I had to consider my options rationally and the decision that logical thought had brought me to, I was strengthened in my resolve to leave my sister's house and her constant glaring at me over breakfast only exacerbated my eagerness to be away from her. I knew there would be consequences to my leaving. With my sister no longer able to criticize every movement of mine, she would turn to criticizing Liza or our father. I needed to ensure that they knew I would not stay away forever. I would visit and they could always come and see me if they found themselves needing out of the house as well. There was also the matter of moving in with the Langleys itself. As generous of an offer as Mr. Langley had made and as understanding as he seemed, I needed to be sure I did not take advantage of his kindness. I would help with the house, clean up after myself, show my gratitude in all things, and make myself available to assist in anything they might need me for. It was the least I could do.

When breakfast was over, I kissed my father on the cheek and Liza on the forehead and hugged them both. I whispered to my sister to visit any time she needed and gave her hand a squeeze as I turned to Victoria. I hugged her too, though she was rather rigid about it, and told her I would visit. She did not respond, only pursed her lips and crossed her arms. Clearly, she was still not going to be supportive of my choice. With a sigh, I heaved my bag onto my shoulder and descended the stairs to the shop below. I waved a goodbye to Benjamin and he waved back, a smile on his face that did not quite reach his eyes.

I called a hansom and rode all the way to Mr. Langley's house, preparing myself for what I was about to do. This was a big step for me and would affect my future in ways I hadn't yet fathomed. I had meant what I said the night before, about how I was too old for men to see me as a viable candidate for marriage. I knew that my logic was sound but my heart had not yet given up on the hope of finding love and having children someday. In time, it would. But at this moment, it saddened me to think of the life I was giving up. Though I had never truly had it.

When I arrived at the Langley's residence, Bernard greeted me as always. Mr. Langley had not been waiting for me outside this morning as I was earlier than usual. Bernard took one look at the bag in my hands and broke into an understanding smile. I smiled kindly back at him.

"Charlotte!" a familiar voice shouted in greeting and I smiled up at Elena Langley. She entered the room at a trot, her beautiful skirts snapping at her heels. She paused in the foyer and took a look at my bag before breaking out into a lovely grin to match Bernard's. "You've accepted! I'm delighted to hear it! You will be the most remarkable companion. Come, I will show you to your rooms. Alexander had them prepared in the hopes that you would accept the post. Bernard, send for the footman to gather the rest of Miss Porter's things."

"Oh," I said, hesitating and glancing at Bernard. "I- there are no more things."

Elena looked down at my meager bag and flushed with embarrassment. "Of course! The only thing a woman like you needs are her wits! That'll be all Bernard, thank you."

She winked at me and walked away, this time heading up the stairs. I hesitated but then followed. I had never been on the second floor of Mr. Langley's home before. The second floor was traditionally reserved for the home's residents, of which I supposed I was now one. Miss Langley led me to a room on the left side of the hall, the first one at the top of the stairs. She threw open the door and marched inside. I paused in the doorway to view my new lodgings. Even this small bedroom was nicer than any I had ever occupied before, even in my childhood home where I had always had to share rooms with my sisters. This one would be all mine. There was a full bed made up with a beautiful patchwork quilt and floral patterned pillows. The sun was streaming in through the thin chiffon curtains. There was a closet, a dresser, an antique mirror, and a small accent chair in the corner. I ran my hands over the fabric of the chair as I looked around me.

My eyes caught at the sight of Mr. Langley. He was standing in the threshold, leaning against the doorframe, long legs crossed at the ankle. He smiled at me, his eyes sparkling with interest.

"Miss Porter," he said in greeting and I nodded my head in response. "I'm delighted you've taken me up on my offer."

"It was very generous, Mr. Langley," I told him, straightening my back and putting as much professionalism into my voice as I could. "I do appreciate it."

"As do I," Elena added, clutching my arm in her own. "Now then, Charlotte, let's get your things unpacked. The sooner we can make you feel at home, the better."

"Thank you, Elena," I said kindly, my eyes sliding from Miss Langley to her brother to find that he was still smiling at me, that strangely wicked grin still upon his face. "But I would like to get to work. My duties have increased now that I will be living here. I do not wish to dally."

Miss Langley did not seem put off at all by my assertion. Rather, she simply backed away from me and nodded, a smile playing at her lips.

"Of course, Charlotte," she said kindly. "Go off on your investigations with Alexander but do not forget that your new post pertains to your companionship with me. I'll expect your company this evening. We have a great deal to talk about."

Her words were commanding but her tone was light and she winked and flashed me one last mischievous grin before slipping past her brother and out into the hallway. I heard her footsteps on the stairs a moment later and wondered just what it was that we had to talk about.

"If you would like to unpack before we begin, I will leave you to it," he said. "Join me in my office when you are ready."

I nodded in thanks and he left me standing in the center of this strange room, wondering how I was to make it feel like home. I took my dresses from my bag and hung them in the closet. There were not many of them, most of my attire having burned up in the fire. I would need to purchase some more when I could spare the money from my father's gambling payments. I set my meager belongings to rights in my new room. It did not take long. Then I ventured out, shutting the door behind me, and down the stairs to Mr. Langley's office. He was alone when I arrived and he quickly set down a folder that he had been looking at when I entered. He pushed it away from him hastily and bid me enter. I did, eying the folder on his desk. It looked suspiciously like the police files we had spent hours investigating only a few nights before but it had elicited such a strange response from Mr. Langley that I knew it could not be one of the same.

"I am suspicious of Mr. Dubois," Mr. Langley said then, drawing my attention back to him.

"As am I," I answered, sitting in the seat across from his desk. He leaned back and watched me, thoughtfully.

"I don't think he has any more of his friend's paintings because I believe he has destroyed them."

"To get to whatever he hid behind their bindings."

"Or to get to whatever Mr. Guillard hid behind their bindings."

I creased my brow. I hadn't considered that possibility.

"They were friends," Mr. Langley explainedlose by all accounts. Mr. Guillard may have hidden something of value in one of his paintings and then told Mr. Dubois about it."

"It would explain why Mr. Dubois would not know which painting it was hidden within. You suspect Mr. Dubois as the thief then?"

"I'm not certain," Mr. Langley said. "There would be other ways to get the paintings. Mr. Dubois is one of the wealthiest men in London. He could simply buy them back under the guise of grief if he wished. There would be no reason to resort to theft."

"The theory of something being hidden behind the bindings was just a theory," I reminded him. "There has been absolutely no evidence of such a thing. In fact, you questioned many of the men about their paintings and none seemed to believe there to be any oddity. If something were behind one of the paintings, it would create a visible bump or would slide around in the framing during movement and make noise. That would have drawn attention from men who sat staring at it for some time."

"True," Mr. Langley said, rubbing his chin contemplatively. "Still I believe we should pursue him as a suspect. Mr. Dubois is a well liked man with many friends. We should speak to them about him. Maybe they are aware of something that transpired between him and Mr. Guillard before the painter's death."

"His suicide, you mean."

"I'm not so certain."

A dark look passed over Mr. Langley's face and a chill went through me. I had suspected the same after learning about the strange conditions of the suicide note but I had not wanted to voice such suspicions. It seemed that now, however, we must.

"You believe he was murdered," I said. It wasn't a question and I did not phrase it as one. Mr. Langley nodded and I took a breath. "Because of the note."

"I would like to get another look at it."

I nodded and my eyes fell on that mysterious folder again.

"What is that?" I asked, gesturing toward the file. Mr. Langley's eyes flashed to it briefly before he waved a hand dismissively. I was not convinced.

"Nothing important," he told me. "Just another case I've been working on. A minor one."

I raised a brow. "Something your partner should perhaps know about?"

"Oh no. I would not concern you with this. It's a simple matter. Should not take much investigation at all," he told me and stood from his desk. I did not like how evasive he was being. "Shall we head to Mr. Dubois'? I would wager one of his myriad of servants may be able to tell us something of the man's character."

I nodded and stood but, when he took a step to walk out from behind the desk, I lunged for the file upon it. He jumped as well but far too late. I gathered the file in my hands and flipped it open. I would feel guilty about invading his privacy later. My curiosity would be insatiable until I discovered what he was hiding. As my eyes roved over the page, my mouth fell open, then my cheeks flamed and I threw the file back onto the desk. I felt rage building up in every inch of my body.

"You retrieved the file on my family's arson?" I snapped, hands on my hips and face burning with anger. Mr. Langley sighed.

"Miss Porter, you are my responsibility now that you work for me and live under my roof. If someone is attempting to hurt you or your family, I have an obligation to look into it."

"You do not," I chided. "I am taking care of it myself and I do not appreciate you going to the police about my family without my knowledge."

"I should have told you," He relented and approached me. I was too furious to back away, however, so I stood my ground. My resolve faltered, though, when he placed his hands on my shoulders and gazed into my eyes with that big blue ocean of his own. "I am sorry. But, Miss Porter, you must let me find the men who did this to your family and hold them responsible. This is what I do, what we do. They don't stand a chance."

He was smiling now, using that devilish charm to win me over. But I refused to succumb. I pushed off from him and headed for the door.

"We will speak about this later," I told him, shooting a glare at him from the threshold. "We have work to do now."

I heard him sigh as he followed after me down the stairs and to the door. A waiting Bernard handed us our things and we thanked him and stepped out into the fresh morning sun. The crisp morning air did nothing to dampen my fury however as we made our way to the coach. The driver greeted us and Mr. Langley told him we would like to return to Mr. Dubois' residence. Then he joined me in the carriage and we rode off for the wealthiest district in London. I did not speak to him as we rode and he did not press me. I glared out of the window the whole ride and took his hand only long enough to be helped from the carriage when we arrived. Mr. Langley said nothing still as we approached the house.

Our knock was answered by the butler who informed us, pleasantly, that his master was not at home. Mr. Langley did not seem perturbed by that at all. In fact, it seemed more suited to our purposes that Mr. Dubois was not home.

"Perhaps we could ask you a few questions then, Mr. Wilkins," Mr. Langley said kindly to the butler. Mr. Wilkins looked from Mr. Langley to me and I offered what I hoped was an encouraging smile.

"About what?" he asked curiously.

"About the artist Guillard. I am very eager to purchase one of his paintings, you see, and Mr. Dubois told me the other day at Mr. Adams house that he had a couple of them here."

Mr. Wilkins' forehead scrunched in apparent confusion.

"He may," he told us. "But I have not seen them. Though most of the staff are not allowed in a few rooms here. His office, for instance."

"Mr. Dubois allows no one in his office?" Mr. Langley asked, surprised. It was, indeed, rather odd. Mr. Wilkins seemed to sense his mistake.

"I am sorry, Mr. Langley, but I am quite unsuitable to discussion on the subject. I know nothing of any Guillard paintings and Mr. Dubois will have to speak with you himself if he wishes to sell them."

"Of course, Mr. Wilkins, I understand that. I am sure Mr. Dubois has many Guillard paintings though it must be difficult for him to consider parting with them. I am told they were good friends."

"Indeed, they were," Mr. Wilkins answered with a sad smile. "Mr. Guillard was a very kind man. Very quiet though. He never spoke much, even to us servants. But Mr. Dubois always seemed delighted by his company. The two of them would spend hours talking in Mr. Dubois' office."

"The office that no one is allowed in?" Mr. Langley questioned with a raised brow and Mr. Wilkins' face turned scarlet.

"I am afraid I will have to ask you to return when Mr. Dubois is home," Mr. Wilkins said, flustered. "Good day, Mr. Langley."

Then he closed the door in our face. I glanced to Mr. Langley expecting to find him upset at the insolence of the butler but, instead, he was smiling. He turned us away from the door and patted me on the arm.

"Very interesting indeed," he muttered under his breath and I imagined it was more of an intonation for himself than meant for me. We were halfway to the carriage when we saw a young boy crossing the expansive yard of Mr. Dubois' residence. He was dirty and wearing clothes two sizes too big and carrying an object in his hand that seemed familiar but that I could not quite place though I was certain it had something to do with horses. I tapped Mr. Langley on the arm and he took my meaning well enough. We crossed the lawn to the boy who now sat on a low marble step, biting into an apple.

"Good morning," I greeted kindly as we approached. The boy glanced up at us with suspicion as he bit into his apple, juice running down his chin as he did.

"Good morning," he answered back, his voice high. I figured him to be around the age of ten.

"Are you a stable boy for Mr. Dubois?" I asked kindly, hoping my sweet tone could in some way pass for maternal instinct.

"I am," he said, eyes darting from me to Mr. Langley. "Who are you?"

"Friends of his," I told him. "We stopped in for a visit but found he was not home."

"He's gone to the gentlemen's club. Had some business there, he said."

"I see. Well, we've been worried about him. He does not seem quite the same since Mr. Vincent Guillard's passing."

The boy stopped chewing then, eyes widening at the mention of the painter. It was a good enough indication to me that he knew something. But I would have to press gently to get him to tell us what that was. Luckily, Mr. Langley seemed to sense that I had this under control and did not say a word behind me.

"Did you know Mr. Guillard?" I asked. The boy shook his head.

"Never met him. Not really. Just saw him around the house and heard what they said about him."

"They?"

"The other servants," He blushed, having been caught eavesdropping.

"I'm sure a boy your age hears a great deal he isn't meant to," I told him. "It's easy to be overlooked when you're small, isn't it?"

I gave him a wink and he smiled, displaying crooked teeth with a gap in the center.

"What did they say about Mr. Guillard?" I asked.

"They talked about his paintings and how he and Mr. Dubois had planned a business to sell them," the boy said and then he looked down suddenly and picked at the fraying edge of his hand me down pants. "And other things."

"You can tell us. We won't tell anyone."

His eyes met mine then and seemed to search them for a moment. I wasn't quite sure what he had thought he found there but it must have been enough to gain his trust because he took a deep breath and steadied himself to tell us what he had overheard.

"Some of the servants said that Mr. Dubois and Mr. Guillard were... together. You know, in that way."

I tried my best to school my features but I had to admit my surprise. Mr. Dubois was every bit the gentleman and was always very kind to me. I had even seen him flirt with women at the auction. But perhaps that had all been a ruse. I had, indeed, thought as much myself when faced with the over the top theatrical flirtation he imbued upon me on our first meeting.

"Thank you for telling us," I said, patting him kindly on the knee. "I can assure you that your secret is safe with us."

He nodded and I stood to my full height. Mr. Langley tipped his hat to the boy and then led me off back down the lawn, toward our awaiting carriage. I opened my mouth to say something but immediately forgot what it was when I noticed the man storming up the small hill toward us. Mr. Langley tightened his grip on my arm and slid himself slightly in front of me in protection as Mr. Dubois approached.

"You again," he said when he reached us. That debonair smile and gentlemanly sophistication had completely vanished from his manner and he was red-faced and disheveled, his black hair falling unceremoniously in front of his face. He pushed it out of the way and turned his glare upon us, particularly Mr. Langley, and I thought that perhaps I should be the one protecting him. "Why are you questioning my servants?"

"We were not questioning them, Mr. Dubois. We were simply having a chat with the stable boy. He's a lovely child and Miss Porter does love children."

Mr. Dubois glanced from Mr. Langley to me and I understood the tactic when I saw the former relax a bit. Mr. Langley was reminding him of a lady's presence and to compose himself without embarrassing him by demanding such an action. It was subtle but not lost on the gentleman who now straightened his collar and cleared his throat.

"Do not speak to my servants without my knowledge again, Mr. Langley," Mr. Dubois said then with far more etiquette, but the fury was still there behind his words. "And I will thank you to stop this harassment."

"Harassment?" I gasped but Mr. Langley only held up his hands in surrender and pulled me along toward the carriage.

"We will not bother you again, Mr. Dubois," he assured him over his shoulder. "Come, Miss Porter, we've got work to do."

Mr. Langley helped me into the carriage but did not say a word until we had pulled safely away from Mr. Dubois' house.

"Do you think it's true?" I asked him, whispering though I wasn't sure why. We were alone in the carriage. It just seemed to be the sort of thing that one whispered. Mr. Langley just shrugged.

"Perhaps it is," he said. "It is none of our business one way or the other."

"No," I agreed. "But it is certainly a secret that one would wish to cover up. Especially in London society."

"I agree that he may perceive it that way," Mr. Langley saidnd Mr. Guillard may have as well."

"But then, what could be hidden in the painting?" I asked, unsure of how this could in any way be connected to the stolen paintings. In truth, I was not certain that it was.

"I would like to view that note again, the real one this time," Mr. Langley said and then he called out to the driver to take us back to the police station and we changed course that moment.

Detectives York and Higgins were not enthusiastic to see us again and reassured us that we were wasting our time even as they retrieved the evidence boxes from the Guillard suicide. Mr. Langley thanked them for their help and their concern and waved them out of the room so that we could get to work. He began to pull things out of the box and examine them. I did the same. I took out the pen that had been found in Mr. Guillard's hand and examined it but it looked like no more than an ordinary pen. The pill bottle revealed even less. It had been prescribed by a doctor to assist Mr. Guillard with his trouble sleeping. That might be a point in favor of the suicide theory. Depressed people oftentimes had difficulty sleeping. I was just about to say so when Mr. Langley spoke first.

"A ledger," he said and I glanced down at the book in his hands. It was a small, leather bound item with names and dates scribbled on every line. There was a monetary amount next to them as well and notes jotted in the margins. A record of sales, it seemed. Mr. Guillard had begun to sell his paintings even before his death it appeared. Though, I noticed, they hadn't fetched nearly the amount that they would after his death. Mr. Langley was gazing down at it, brow creased in thought. "Wait a moment."

He rifled through the box again and pulled out the suicide note. He set it beside the ledger, eyes darting back and forth. I noticed it at the same time he did and let out a gasp of my own as he sat back and bit his lip, a curious look on his face. He tapped a finger over one of the letters in the note and stood. I gazed down at it. It was the letter Y but the tail had a curl in it. Every Y in the note had a curl in it. I glanced to the ledger. Mr. Roger Tiffany. His name did not have a curl in the Y. The handwriting did not match. Someone else had written Mr. Guillard's suicide note.

12 Companions

Mr. Langley thought it best that we admit our suspicions to no one until such time as they could be verified. I quite agreed and so we packed up the box of Mr. Guillard's belongings and evidence from the crime scene that had just become a murder and gave it back to the detectives before turning to leave the police station. We were stopped, however, before we could reach the door by the appearance of a familiar constable.

"Miss Porter," he said and I turned to see the man who had taken my statement the night that my father was threatened by thugs and our shop burned to the ground. His eyes strayed from mine to the man whose arm was linked with my own. "Are you here about the arson? Or the threats? Have there been more?"

"Threats?" Mr. Langley raised a brow as he looked to me.

"No, constable," I assured him with a smile, trying my best not to let my irritation show through my tone. After all, he could not possibly know how very much I did not want to talk about the matter at present. "Thank you for your concern."

I made an effort to steer Mr. Langley away from the constable and toward the door but he did not budge. The man could be infuriating when he had a mind to be.

"Have you made any progress in your investigation?" Mr. Langley asked, his voice sounding oddly strained. I looked up at his face to see the vein in his neck throbbing.

"I'm afraid we have not," the constable said. There was a pain in his voice, the sound of regret. It caught me off guard. He wrung his hands together and stared at me as though he had something to say. I waited. "Miss Porter, I want to apologize for not taking your statement seriously. Your father did not seem to want to report the incident and I chalked it up to some local thugs wanting to steal from your family's shop. But when I heard about the fire and how you risked your life, I thought-"

"Risked her life?" Mr. Langley's gaze fell to me, his eyes widened in surprise. I closed my own and took a breath. I hadn't wanted to endure this lecture.

"I should not have allowed you to leave the station and return home without an escort," the constable forged on. "To allow a young woman out on these streets alone after dark... it was my responsibility as a lawman to see you home safely. If I had done that-"

"The fire was not your fault, constable," I said kindly, hoping to assuage his guilt and remove myself from this conversation as soon as possible. "It is the fault of those thugs who threatened my father. But all is well now. We have moved on and are saving money to rebuild the shop. Please do not trouble yourself over it any longer."

I turned on my heel then and pulled Mr. Langley away toward the door. I had lied about saving money to rebuild. We were scraping together some money but it was not to rebuild. But I had learned my lesson about involving the police in the business of my father's debt and would not risk the lives of my family again. Nor would I risk Victoria's home or, God forbid, the Langley's. I had no idea of how far these thugs would go to secure their investment but I did not intend to test them.

"I will try my best to find the men who did this to your family, Miss Porter, mark my words," the constable called out behind us. He meant them as a comfort but I gritted my teeth against them. Going to the police had been what set the thugs upon us in the first place. I hoped, for my family's sake, that the constable was as inept at his job as he seemed.

I said nothing to Mr. Langley as we entered the carriage but he seemed certain not to let this go.

"What did he mean that you risked your life, Miss Porter?" Mr. Langley asked when we were comfortably settled in and on our way home. I sighed. Realizing that he would not let this go until he had heard the story in its entirety, I settled in for the ride and for the telling of the tale he so desperately wanted to hear.

"Two thugs came into my father's shop and threatened him that night. When I went to discover what the commotion was about, one of them held a knife to my throat and threatened me as well," I told him, plunging into my story, hoping to finish it up as soon as I could and end this line of questioning. Mr. Langley's jaw hardened at the notion of my having a knife to my throat but I forged on. "My younger sister, Liza, fetched a constable but the thugs were gone by the time he arrived. So I journeyed with the constable, that man who has just spoken to us, back to the police station to file a report on the incident despite my father's protests that I should do no such thing. I did not understand at the time that he feared retaliation if we should go to the police. I did not understand that he was in debt to those men and how dangerous they could be. By the time I returned from the police station, the shop was ablaze. The neighbors were outside watching it burn but I saw no trace of my father or my sister. I reasoned that they must still be inside so I... I ran into the building."

"You ran into a burning building?" he asked and I gulped. I knew what I had done was foolish and, for some reason, I hated the idea of disappointing him.

"I found them huddled behind the printing press. I helped them out and we all escaped unscathed. We watched the shop burn to embers and then, with nowhere else to go, we left for my sister's house that evening."

I concluded the tale and stared down at my hands. I did not want to hear the lecture that I knew was coming but I steeled myself for it anyway. I was stunned, then, when Mr. Langley reached forward and grasped my hands in his own. The gesture was so intimate that it forced me to look up into his eyes. There was no anger there, not like there had been before when he discovered that I had not told him about the arson. Instead, there was a sadness. It was not pity, not truly, but perhaps sympathy.

"That was very brave of you," he told me and I blinked in surprise.

"You don't think me foolish?" I asked and he smiled.

"We all do foolish things when it comes to the people we love," he told me, releasing my hands and sitting back in his seat. I was almost sad at the loss of contact but straightened myself up as he continued, gazing out of the window in contemplation. "I imagine I would have done the same thing."

I settled myself in for the ride back to Mr. Langley's home and, I supposed, what was now my residence as well. It was not a long journey and before I knew it, Mr. Langley was helping me down from the carriage with a smile. We entered the house and said our hellos to Bernard who took our hats and gloves and then whispered. "Miss Langley is entertaining visitors in the drawing room."

"Friends of hers?" Mr. Langley asked and Bernard raised a brow.

"I don't think so, sir."

Curiosity got the best of me and I followed Mr. Langley to the drawing room despite the fact that it was most likely more appropriate for me to excuse myself to my rooms so that the Langleys could entertain their guests. I entered the drawing room right behind Mr. Langley to find his mother returned with yet another pair of women. This time, however, it was not Mrs. and Miss Walsh who greeted us but rather the very familiar Mrs. Herbert and what was apparently her daughter, Miss Herbert. Elizabeth Herbert had inherited most of her mother's features, the blonde hair and pouty lips. She was quite stunning, I had to admit, and she turned the full force of her radiant smile upon Mr. Langley the moment we entered. I remained behind him, planted firmly by the door.

"Alexander," Mrs. Langley exclaimed as he entered and Mr. Langley moved forward to hug his mother. As he did, he met Elena's eyes over the woman's shoulder and his sister gave him the smallest shake of the head. I was not sure quite what that meant but I was certain that I was the only one to have seen it. When Mr. Langley separated from his mother, she held him firmly in her grasp as she turned him to face the guests. "This is Mrs. Penelope Herbert, whom I am told you have met, and her daughter, the lovely Miss Elizabeth Herbert."

"Mrs. Herbert," he began politely. "A pleasure to see you again. And Miss Herbert, a delight to meet you."

The girl's smile broadened and she batted her eyes up at him. It took the full force of my willpower not to snort. Elena cast an eye to me and a mischievous smile touched her lips. I returned it. Perhaps I was not the only one aware of and amused by Miss Herbert's obvious ploy.

"It's lovely to meet you as well, sir," She spoke delicately, like a well bred lady, much unlike the way he was used to my accosting him or his sister commanding him. Miss Herbert was the very picture of a demure, elegant lady, a quality that many men looked for in a wife. It would serve her well. "My mother told me of your kindness when she met you the other night. I could not wait to meet you for myself."

Mr. Langley smiled kindly. "I did tell your mother that you were always welcome visitors."

She blushed at that and I stared in awe. I had never known before that it was possible to blush on command. Perhaps it would be possible to make yourself avoid blushing as well. I could certainly use that skill. The silence was palpable as Miss Herbert gazed up at a slightly uncomfortable Mr. Langley. I thought perhaps I could spare him at least one moment of the awkwardness. I cleared my throat and all eyes fell on me. Mrs. Herbert's derision was clear upon her otherwise elegant face.

"If you'll excuse me," I said with a curtsy. Mr. Langley bit his lip at that. He did not seem to care for my recognition that this room was full of women who ranked far above me. But it was the appropriate thing to do. As were the words I was about to speak next. "I will leave you to your guests, Mr. Langley. Mrs. Herbert, it was lovely to see you again. Miss Herbert, so nice to meet you."

Though she had never introduced herself to me. I turned and began to exit. Bernard opened the door so that I could but Mr. Langley was suddenly in front of me and I found myself quite unable to escape.

"Stay, Miss Porter, I insist," he told me, his eyes sparkling with mischief as he gazed into my own. "You have no need to excuse yourself. This being your home as well."

I clenched my jaw as he smirked, wishing he hadn't said such a thing. I heard a twin pair of gasps behind me and turned to see Mrs. and Miss Herbert looking positively scandalized. Elena used a hand to hide her smile and Mrs. Langley just narrowed her gaze at the two of us standing in the threshold.

"What do you mean this is her home as well, Alexander?" his mother queried carefully. "Do you mean to tell me she lives here?"

"She does."

He said nothing more. I wished he would.

"She is my companion," Elena spoke up then and I wanted to hug her in gratitude. "She assists Alexander during the day and keeps me company in the evening. We are going to a show on Friday."

She crossed the room and took my arm, tucking it into her own. Then she led me back to the chair she sat in and pushed me into it with her. We squeezed together so closely that I knew it could not be comfortable for her but I also knew that she was making a point to protect me and I appreciated it. I also hoped that her efforts would not go unnoticed as my duties as her companion would, hopefully, distance me from Mr. Langley in their minds. Mrs. and Miss Herbert seemed to be making their mind up about whether or not I was a threat to their true purpose here, gazing from me to Mr. Langley and back. I noticed that he was still watching me, those bright blue eyes sparkling. I wished he wouldn't. Mrs. Langley seemed to have recovered her composure sooner than the rest of them as usual and she smoothed her skirt out with her hands before smiling at me.

"Well," she said, her voice the most kind that I had ever heard it. "If your presence in this house gets Elena out of it more often than I do believe I owe you a great deal of gratitude. She seems more excited for this season than any other, more willing to put herself out there. If it is you that I have to thank for that development, then I thank you, Miss Porter."

She went so far as to place a hand on my arm and meet my gaze with a warm smile.

"You're very kind, Mrs. Langley."

It was all I could manage given the strange difference in her mannerisms. I was grateful that she had chosen to be kind to me but I was not certain that it extended beyond the obligatory pleasantries she was paying me. I was, in no way, responsible for Miss Langley's return to the London social scene but, if she wanted to believe it and Elena did not want to correct her, I would not argue with any goodwill it gained in my favor.

"Mr. Langley," Miss Herbert said then, turning the conversation away from me and drawing attention to herself as she had hoped. I was not offended. I could breathe a bit better when the eyes of these scrutinizing women were not upon me. Miss Langley gave me a small squeeze of encouragement as Miss Herbert continued. "I hear you have been in America for the past three years."

"I have," Mr. Langley answered, taking up a position leaning against the mantle. He gazed down at all of us and we gazed right back. Five women. I almost felt bad for him.

"I hear it's a beautiful country."

"It is. The environment is different depending on where you go, of course. I spent most of my time in California, near the desert. It's beautiful country."

Miss Herbert's lips parted in awe as she nodded to every word of his story. Miss Langley elbowed me and I looked up at her to see her roll her eyes. I smirked. Mr. Langley caught the action out of the corner of his eye and smiled at us.

"What were you doing there?" Miss Herbert blurted before she could phrase it better. She was attempting to draw Mr. Langley's attention back to her as she had noticed it had shifted. Her mother had noticed as well and shot us a glare from her position on the sofa. I looked down at my lap.

"I was there on business," Mr. Langley answered. His voice sounded more curt than it had before. "My father and I were considering investing in some American products."

"How fascinating. Did you-"

"Dinner, Mr. Langley," Bernard said, appearing in the doorway. Mr. Langley nodded at the butler and gestured for us to head across the hall to the dining room. Miss Langley gave my arm a squeeze before looping her own with her mother's and leading the way to the dining room. Mrs. and Miss Herbert followed after them, looped together as well. I exited the drawing room and made a move for the stairs but Mr. Langley caught my arm in his grip and I turned around to face him.

"You aren't leaving me to suffer through this alone, are you?" he asked, his crooked smile in place.

"You have Elena," I answered, prying his fingers off of my arm. "And you have your mother. Whom I quite believe would rather I was not present at this dinner."

"It isn't my mother's decision," he told me. "And I want you there."

The intensity in his eyes stunned me into silence and shattered any argument I may have had. I could do nothing more than walk off into the dining room when he gestured for me to go ahead. The women had been speaking to one another before but that changed when I entered. They all gazed at me in surprise, all but Elena who smirked victoriously from her seat next to her mother. I lowered my head as my cheeks flamed and made my way to the seat next to Elena. Unfortunately, Mr. Langley chose the seat beside me. Though that could have been more due to the fact that it was the head of the table and next to Miss Herbert as well. Though Elizabeth Herbert did not seem to believe that to be the case and she glared at me as the servants brought out the first course.

"Thank you Maggie," I said as the woman set the plate before me. The pretty cook beamed at me and gave my arm a gentle squeeze before heading back to the kitchen. I smiled as I turned to face my meal but noticed that everyone was staring at me. I shifted uncomfortably in my seat as I took in the surprise on the faces around me. Even Elena looked surprised but hers faded first and was replaced by a smile. Only Mr. Langley smiled my way, a hint of amusement playing at his lips. Perhaps these people were above calling the servants by their names but I was not. I was no different from them, after all. We were of the same class. Many of the neighborhood children that I had grown up with had found service in the wealthy's employ. So, despite the stares now directed my way, I refused to be embarrassed. Luckily, Elena came to the rescue, sensing my unease and the tension in the room.

"Alexander just purchased that painting on the wall behind you the other evening, Elizabeth. Isn't it breathtaking?"

The Herberts turned to admire the art and the conversation shifted to the subject. I breathed a sigh of relief and turned my attention to my meal, stuffing my mouth to keep myself quiet. I had never dined so elegantly before and I stared down at the fresh bread and jam as though I were expecting to wake from a dream at any moment. Miss Langley smiled at me and I began to eat with the rest of them, remembering the manners that my mother had instilled in me as a child so that I would know how to behave around the upper class customers who had begun to visit our shop.

The dinner passed by rather uneventfully and in the same vein as the conversation in the drawing room. Miss Herbert flipped her hair and batted her eyelashes and asked Mr. Langley all manner of questions, most of which were not exactly of the manner in which would begin a conversation of any kind. Mr. Langley answered politely but never very eagerly. Mrs. Langley tried to engage Mrs. Herbert in conversation but the latter seemed far more interested in the progress her daughter was making with Mr. Langley. Miss Langley elbowed me and rolled her eyes time and time again and every time, I would smile at her and try my hardest not to giggle at her indications. Mr. Langley noticed once or twice and would smirk in our direction briefly before Miss Herbert would rush on with another question or a story of her own and he would be forced to return his attention to her.

By the end of dinner, I felt rather exhausted and quite ready to retire. I sat in the drawing room while Mr. and Miss Langley saw their visitors and their mother out and waved as they got into their separate carriages and rode off. Then I rose to inform them that I would be retiring and bid them goodnight but, before I could, I heard their raised voices in the foyer.

"She positively threw herself at you," Miss Langley said the moment they were gone.

"You are the one who allowed her in," he answered.

"How could I not when you practically gave her mother an invitation at that auction of yours?" Miss Langley spat back and I heard their footsteps approaching the drawing room. They entered and I froze in place, unsure of how to excuse myself from the presence of this familial argument. Surely, they would stop and give me the chance. But they did not. Elena turned to her brother. "You knew this was going to happen, Alexander. I warned you that it would. Mother cannot leave well enough alone and she will not stop now that you've returned from America."

"I know," he said with a sigh. He ran a hand through his hair and sounded more exhausted than I had ever heard him. "I know how bad it was for you when I was gone."

"She will do the same to you now. I appreciate you allowing me to stay in the city with you, Alexander, truly I do. But believe me when I say she will not stop until we are both wed. No matter where we go or what we do, she will continue to drag men and women to this house until one of us says I do."

"I know," he said again. "I will speak with her about it."

"Perhaps you can get through to her. Every time I try to speak with her about it, we only shout at each other."

He smiled. "You are two very headstrong women."

"And you've always known how to handle the both of us," Miss Langley said, her voice softening as she touched her brother's arm. "Do it quickly, Alexander. She will not stop pushing women upon you until you do."

"I wish she wouldn't."

Perhaps it was the night of holding in my laughter but I found that too amusing to bite back my chuckle. They both turned to me then and I immediately regretted my snort.

"Is that funny, Miss Porter?" Mr. Langley asked then, raising an eyebrow and smiling.

"Indeed it is," I answered. "In my experience, most men would die to have women clamoring all over them."

Elena barked out a laugh at that and Mr. Langley's smile widened, revealing his perfect teeth. Miss Langley left him standing in the doorway and crossed the room to me. She looped her arm through my own once more and guided me back onto the sofa.

"If that's all, Alexander, do leave me to spend some time with my new companion," Miss Langley said, smiling at her brother. "After a night of such dreadful company, I am eager for some of Miss Porter's sparkling wit."

He looked between us and then nodded.

"As you wish," he said and then made a mock bow to the both of us before exiting the drawing room. I heard him ascending the stairs a moment later.

"Did I not tell you that Elizabeth Herbert was a bore?" Miss Langley said the moment he was gone, a sigh of exasperation escaping her lips as she did. "And rather unremarkable. You saw that for yourself tonight."

"She does not have the penchant for conversation," I admitted. "But I thought she was rather beautiful. Not as beautiful as you though, Elena."

She laughed at that.

"You think my dislike of her is because of envy?" she asked and I felt my eyes grow wide in the realization of how she had taken my comment.

"No!" I exclaimed. "Of course not. You have nothing to envy of her. I was only being truthful. She is very pretty but you are much more so."

"I suppose that perhaps I was referring to inner beauty anyway," Miss Langley brushed it off with a wave of her hand and leaned back in her seat as she did. "She is quite the ugly person. Her and Miss Walsh both."

"Truly? Why do you say that?"

Elena bit her lip and glanced to the door as if concerned that we would be overheard.

"I had a friend," she said. "last season. Her name was Anne Withersby. She was a wonderful woman. Kind and generous and demure. She was not the most beautiful woman in London but she was so giving. She volunteered at the orphanage on most weekends. Can you believe that? Anyway, we became close very quickly and attended everything together. Eventually, I began to get the idea that I should arrange for a meeting between her and my brother when he returned as I knew he would be coming home soon. She was shy about it at first and declined, saying she did not want to take advantage of my friendship. That was the kind of person she was, you see. So I convinced her that she was not taking advantage of my friendship but that if it worked out with my brother we could be sisters."

I nodded along and Miss Langley turned to me to continue.

"Well, we arranged for her to meet my brother the moment he arrived home. I even wrote to him to tell him about her and he said he would be delighted to meet her. Well, some of the other eligible women heard of our plan. Felicity Walsh and Elizabeth Herbert were just two of them but they were the leaders of the pack. They have had their eyes on Alexander since we were children and they were not about to let shy little Anne Withersby stand in their way. So they..."

She trailed off here and I saw that the corners of her eyes were watering. I stood and gathered a handkerchief from the side cabinet. I handed it to her and she thanked me, dabbing her eyes with it as she continued.

"They ruined her, Charlotte," she told me, her words coming out in a rush of emotion. "They spread a rumor that Anne had a dalliance with a man from France. They got a bunch of other women to say it too and soon it was all anyone could talk about. I tried to defend Anne but they accused me of lying to protect her and Anne ran off crying. The next day, her things were gone from her parents' house and they told me that she had moved to the country where she could be away from the vicious rumors. I didn't hear from her for months and then she wrote to me to tell me that she had joined a convent. A convent! Can you imagine, Charlotte? She will never marry, never bear children, all because those wretched girls ruined her name."

Elena sniffled at the memory and I placed a comforting hand on her shoulder but my mind was spinning with the information. So this was why Mr. Langley had expressed no interest in Miss Walsh or Miss Herbert. It was not that he had no desire to marry. It was that he had no desire to marry them. He knew of their true character through the experience of his sister. I thought of Anne Withersby as well, a ruined reputation forcing her into the life of a nun. I thought about it for a moment. The convent life did not seem terrible. The dedication of one's mind, body, and soul to God was a valiant decision, regardless of her reasons. Still, she should have been allowed her options. If she had, would she be married to Mr. Langley today? If that were the case, I would be out of a job. I patted Miss Langley on the shoulder and she smiled over to me.

"I think about Anne often," she confessed. "One day, I'm going to visit her. But she's just one example of how cruel this city of ours can be. Especially to women."

I nodded. She didn't have to tell me about the cruelty of London society. I may not have nearly the weight upon my shoulders that Miss Langley did. I may not have to put up with the snobby London elite whispering about me behind my back and smiling at me to my face but there were expectations in the lower classes as well. Marrying by a certain age, assisting husbands in their shops, completing duties of the home. In the lower classes, much like in the upper, a woman's value was precisely equal to the number of children that she had come by legitimately. At twenty five, my chance at that number dwindled by the day and I had not yet decided whether or not I believed that to be a bad thing. Still, I would be judged by it all the same.

"I think it's wrong," she continued. "This system of ours. How the wealthy marry the wealthy out of duty and title. But you know my feelings on the matter. I'm curious about yours."

"Mine?" I asked, surprised by the blatant request. She smiled.

"You've seen an example of the marriage trade just tonight. What do you think of it?"

"I think..." I thought for a moment. I did not want to say something to offend her but I also did not want to lie. "I think that everyone has the right to be happy. Ideally, we could all choose who to marry based upon who we love. But that is not the way that things work. And I'm no expert on love myself."

"Have you ever been in love?"

An image of my ex-fiancé's face floated in my vision. But that was not love. That was duty as well.

"No," I answered and her face fell.

"We will," she assured me, patting my leg gently. "Both of us will fall in love. Someday we will,"

13 An Understanding

T he next day I awoke and was surprised, at first, to find myself in the strange room with unfamiliar surroundings. But then slowly my brain became aware of the memory that I had moved into this house just the previous day. I rose and dressed. I brushed my hair and pulled it up, made my bed with the homely quilts, and smoothed out the pillows. Then I descended the stairs for breakfast. I peered into Mr. Langley's office to see if he was already at work and if I should make a rush of my breakfast to join him but he was not there. He was not in the drawing room or the dining room either.

I found Bernard chatting happily with Maggie in the kitchen. This was a room that I had not been in before. It was large, boasting a sizable stove and quite a bit of counter space and pantries. Maggie leaned against one now, sipping her tea and smiling at the laughing Bernard who held a cup of his own. I paused to admire the scene for a moment. It was the most lifelike I had ever seen the servants. Maggie muttered something else and Bernard burst into a fresh bit of laughter. I smiled at the sound of the deep chuckle. Then Maggie's eyes slid to the side and she saw me. She sat down her tea immediately, wiping her hands on her apron and clearing her throat. Bernard turned to see me and turned stoic as well.

"Don't stop on my account," I said kindly, taking a step forward. "I wasn't aware that Bernard was capable of laughter."

Maggie chuckled at that. Bernard smiled.

"Miss Porter," Bernard nodded in greeting. "What can we do for you?"

"You can call me Charlotte, Bernard," I told him. "Seeing as I'm an employee of Mr. Langley's as well."

Bernard and Maggie exchanged a glance that I did not quite understand but it culminated in a shrug from the latter as she stepped toward me.

"Would you like some tea dear?" she asked, crossing behind me to the kettle.

"That would be lovely. Might I ask what was so amusing?"

"The chicken's gotten out again," Maggie said, good humoredly, as she poured my tea. Bernard smirked as he sipped his own. I took the cup from her once it was poured and perched myself against the counter beside them. "Harold's been trying to catch it all morning."

"Harold?"

"Another servant," she told me with a smile. "Your carriage driver."

"Ah," I answered, embarrassed that I had not asked for the boy's name sooner. I said it again now to commit it to memory. "Harold."

"You and Mr. Langley have been putting him to work quite a bit lately," Bernard said, eying me over his spectacles as he sipped his tea. I frowned.

"I do hope we aren't exhausting the poor boy," I responded. "I could convince Mr. Langley to walk from time to time. Most of the men we are visiting for our current case live within the wealthy district as well so-"

"It's not a bother at all, dear," Maggie said with a wave of her hand. "Harold loves driving the carriage. As much as he loves working for Mr. Langley."

Bernard nodded at the sentiment. It seemed Mr. Langley had the love of his employees. That was good to know. I was not certain how long Bernard, Maggie, and Harold had been in his employ but they seemed more than happy to remain so. That boded well for a new hire such as myself.

"Speaking of our employer," I said. "Where is he this morning?"

"Mr. Langley has gone into town this morning to handle some business. I should have told you sooner. He asked me to tell you that he will return this afternoon for you to continue your work on the investigation."

I nodded and thanked the dutiful butler.

"For now," Maggie said, eyes cast to the ceiling when she heard footsteps above us. "It appears the mistress of the house is nearly ready for her breakfast. I imagine she will want her companion to join her."

I nodded and set my tea cup down. I thanked Maggie for it and thanked both she and Bernard for the conversation before leaving them behind in the kitchen to take my seat in the dining room beyond. I was joined, not long after, by a yawning Miss Langley. We had stayed up rather late in the evening discussing love and friends and family and anything else we could manage. It had been an enjoyable time. I was beginning to like Elena Langley immensely and was grateful for that as it would make my companionship with her far easier.

We ate and talked some more and then moved into the drawing room where we worked on some embroidery and chatted about the London gossip. She told me about the scandals of the upper echelons and I told her about the rumors of the lower class. It was well past noon, if the clock on the mantel was any indication, when the front door burst open and Bernard came running into the foyer. We could hear the grunts and shouts of indignation from the entryway as we set our embroidery down and ran into the hall to see what was the matter. My hands flew to my mouth to cover my gasp when I saw the scene awaiting us.

Bernard held the door open, his mouth agape, as Mr. Harrison helped Mr. Langley into the house. The latter had his arm around the former's shoulders and looked up at Elena and I with a look of fury. It faded at the sight of us but I felt my own rising within me. His left eye was entirely swollen closed and dark purple all around it. Elena ran forward to help Mr. Harrison and peered closely at the injury when she had reached her brother's side. Mr. Langley did not fight the attention, allowing her to hold his head firmly in her hands and examine the injury, but his eyes found mine and his lips lifted into a gruesome smile. Gruesome only because of the bloody cut marring his lower lip.

"You should see the other guy," he said in jest but he had exceptionally misread the mood of the room.

"What happened, Alexander?" Miss Langley was shouting, concerned and appalled, as she placed a finger gently to his eye and he flinched. "Who did this to you?"

"You did not go out to handle business, did you?" I snapped, my hands on my hips. Elena turned to look at me and then back to her brother, confusion plain on her face. Mr. Harrison's face sobered and his eyes turned away from me.

"In a way," he answered with a smirk in my direction.

"Oh no you don't," I admonished. "You are not smirking your way out of this. Mr. Harrison, please help Mr. Langley to the drawing room. Bernard, fetch us some ice for Mr. Langley's eye. Elena, stop fussing over it. You will only irritate it more."

They all fell in line at my commands, I was shocked to see. But my surprise was overshadowed by my fury and I marched into the drawing room ahead of them all. I waited as Mr. Harrison sat Mr. Langley on the couch. Bernard ran back in with the ice and gave it to Elena who sat at his side and touched the ice to his eye. Mr. Langley winced at the pain. Good. I crossed my arms and glared at him through narrowed eyes.

"You went to the East End," I told him. It wasn't a question. He did not deny it. "What were you thinking?"

"I was investigating," he told me with a sigh.

"The men there did not appreciate it," Mr. Harrison told me. So he had been there as well. At least I could take some solace in the fact that Mr. Langley had not been stupid enough to go alone. "They did this to him for 'asking too many questions' or so they said."

I felt my jaw clench.

"I told you to let me handle this," I reminded him, anger in every word.

"I don't want you going to that place!" Mr. Langley snapped. He pushed Elena's hand away and rose to his feet, glaring at me through his one good eye. The effect was markedly diminished. "If they did this to me, I would not want to think of what they might do to you!"

Mr. Harrison and Miss Langley gaped at me and the indication that I had been going somewhere unsavory. I felt heat rising to my cheeks.

"I am not your responsibility!" I shouted at him. I knew I should not. He was my employer and I was toeing a thin line. But in my fury, I could not help myself. "You are my employer. You have no personal hold on me! I can do as I wish in my own time!"

"You don't even know how much danger you are in!"

"I am perfectly aware of the danger, thank you. Might I remind you what happened the last time the authorities got involved? You going there and asking questions will drum up nothing but trouble for me and my family. I have to protect them!"

My words were coming out less in anger and more as a pleading. It surprised even me. I was furious, that had not changed. But it sounded, even to my own ears, that I was begging him not to get involved more than I was ordering him to. That made sense. I could not force Mr. Langley to do anything any more than he could force me not to but I could plead with him, get him to understand the danger that he was putting my family in and how I could not abide by it.

"You do not have to do it alone," he told me then, his tone softening. He took a step toward me but I backed away. I was still shaking from my anger and I did not want to risk what I might say or do if I remained here a moment longer. Especially if he were attempting to get closer to me. "Miss Porter-"

"No," I interrupted him. Then I stormed from the room and to the foyer. I gestured to Bernard and he ran off to gather my hat and gloves. "It is afternoon and we have work to do. We will discuss it once we are finished."

Then I was out the door and heading for the carriage, pulling on my gloves as I went. I helped myself inside and sat waiting in the seat, taking deep breaths to calm myself. Mr. Langley joined me a short time later, holding the ice to his eye with one hand. It kept slipping from the cloth that it was wrapped in and he struggled to wrap it back up, squinting at it with his one good eye. After a moment, I sighed and slid over next to him to help. I pulled the cloth gently from his fingers and wrapped the ice tightly inside. Then I pressed it tenderly to his eye. He turned to look at me with the other.

"I'm sorry, Miss Porter," he said then and I knew he meant it. "I know that you are under a lot of pressure to help your family but these people, the ones who your father owes debt to, they deserve to pay for what they did to you."

I felt tears welling up in my eyes at my own sense of injustice but I stood my ground as I spoke. "I will pay my father's debt and then they will leave us alone."

"They won't," he told me and something flashed in his eyes. I felt my shoulders drop. "You know that, don't you? You know how those sort of men do their business. They find someone like your father, a helpless addict, and get him indebted to them. And then they make it impossible for him to pay his debts. You've made the first payment, Miss Porter. But they will increase the interest and demand more. Ask your father. I'm sure they had already tried the same trick on him before you learned of it."

"How do you know that?" I asked. I heard my voice shaking as I did. He sighed.

"I've seen it happen before," he told me. "Time and time again. To good men and decent families. They won't stop. You will never pay them off and they will never stop being a threat to you. Unless..."

He touched my hand and looked into my eyes.

"Unless you allow me to get them put away for arson."

I stared at him, considering what he had said. Somehow, I knew he was right. My father had been gambling for over a year. He had been making payments. He had to have been, otherwise those thugs would have shown up at our door much sooner. So they must have already grown too much for him to bear. Perhaps Mr. Langley was right. Perhaps they would never stop and my family would never be free of them. Perhaps allowing him to investigate the arson was the only way to be rid of them. I closed my eyes and sighed. Then I nodded.

"I will not go on my own anymore," he promised me, squeezing my hand as he did. "You can be as involved as you want to be. I promise."

"And we will do it quietly," I added as a condition. "So that they don't know."

"I promise."

I nodded again as the carriage came to a stop. We exited the carriage to find ourselves back in front of Mr. Adams' house. Mr. Langley knocked and we were greeted by the butler who left to find Mr. Adams at once. The older gentleman joined us in a matter of minutes, smiling as he did.

"Mr. Langley," he greeted. "Miss Porter. To what do I owe the pleasure?"

"The last time we were here, you said that Mr. Dubois had written to you asking to stop in to see your painting," Mr. Langley began. "Would you happen to still have that letter?"

Mr. Adams gazed at us curiously for a moment, his gaze lingering on Mr. Langley's strange black eye, an injury a gentleman was not likely to have, before answering. "I may still have it in my office, I suppose. Why do you ask?"

"Could we see it?"

Mr. Adams' forehead creased in confusion but after a moment he shrugged and led the way to his office, having obviously decided that our strange request could cause no harm. We entered the office and waited patiently as Mr. Adams sorted through the various correspondence on his desk for a few minutes. After a while, he pulled a letter out and slid it across the desk to us.

"There it is, Mr. Langley," he told us. "Can't say that it contains any interesting information at all. Just that he would be stopping by to see the painting."

I gazed at the letter over Mr. Langley's shoulder and silently gave thanks that every day of the week had the letter Y in it as I saw the familiar curl on the letter's tip.

"Thank you, Mr. Adams," Mr. Langley said, handing the letter back to him so calmly that, had I not known any better, I would have thought we had found nothing at all. "You've been most helpful. I know it was a strange request but I thank you for your compliance. We must follow any possible lead in this investigation, you see. No matter how ludicrous it may seem."

"I understand," Mr. Adams answered and then he saw us out, bidding us a good day as he did. Mr. Langley returned the favor and then helped me back into the carriage. I was nearly bursting when he climbed in beside me.

"That connects Mr. Dubois to the murder of Mr. Guillard," I said excitedly as the carriage rode off.

"It's not enough," Mr. Langley told me, pressing the partially melted ice back to his injured eye.

"Not enough?" I asked curiously. "I've seen men hang for less."

"Not men like him. Not one of the wealthiest men in London," He sighed. "We need to connect it all to the paintings. We have to tie him directly to the murder, one way or another. A curled Y is not going to be enough to convince a judge."

The carriage came to a stop again and we were back home. It was not a far ride from Mr. Langley's house to Mr. Adams', both of them being men of means living in the same area of London. Mr. Langley helped me from the carriage and followed me into the house. Bernard nodded in the direction of the drawing room and I turned to see a familiar face. Chief Detective Ryland stood, fully uniformed, in the drawing room.

"Chief Detective Ryland," Mr. Langley said as he entered. "a pleasure to see you again."

"You as well, Mr. Langley. What happened to your eye? Did you get into a fight with another gentleman about some investments?"

He smiled at his teasing. Mr. Langley smiled back.

"Something like that," Mr. Langley answered. "What can I do for you?"

"Another painting was stolen," he said then and Mr. Langley cast a glance my way.

"Whose?"

"Mr. Randall Dabner. He said that you and Miss Porter had warned him that someone might be trying to steal it. He wanted you there for the investigation. My men are at the crime scene now."

"Well, let's join them then, shall we?"

Just like that, we were headed right back out to the coach. I thought about poor Harold in the driver's seat and shot him a smile as Mr. Langley helped me into the carriage. He smiled back but his eyes showed his shock. Chief Detective Ryland joined us as well and we made our way to 142 Park Lane in haste. The house was swarmed with constables and detectives already upon our arrival. We entered through the front door and made our way into Mr. Dabner's study. The man himself was there, speaking to Detective Higgins who did not look pleased to see us. Mr. Dabner stopped speaking with him immediately and approached us.

"You must find whoever did this," he said in a frenzy. "It isn't right. It's not... natural."

Mr. Langley started to ask him what he meant but stopped just as suddenly. My gaze followed his to see precisely what Mr. Dabner was referring to. The painting which had hung so pleasantly on the wall behind his desk had not been stolen as Chief Detective Ryland had thought. It had been cut open, sliced clean through, the binding visible for all to see.

14 Addiction

"When did this happen?" Mr. Langley was asking the distressed Mr. Dabner who seemed far more interested in stomping furiously and frantically about his office, ensuring that none of his other possessions had gone missing as well. He did not appear to have heard my employer's question and Mr. Langley had to repeat it as the man rifled through his own desk drawers looking for only he knew what.

"Sometime last night, I suppose. I don't know. I was away," Mr. Dabner answered, brushing off Mr. Langley's question as inconsequential, shutting one drawer and moving to the next.

I made my way to the torn canvas on the wall and leaned forward to inspect it. It was a terrible thing, to destroy art in such a way, especially art that could never be replaced now that the artist himself was deceased. Colorful strips hung pathetically from the canvas frame but it was the frame itself that held my interest at the moment. I inspected it for any signs of tampering. It was a common, albeit cheaply made, wooden stapled frame. It was precisely what one would expect to see behind a canvas painting. If something had been removed, I was unable to tell. The paper backing was perfectly in place and did not appear to have ever been removed. Though a skilled framer could have done so without leaving a trace. There was nothing remarkable at all about this particular painting and I began to turn away from it when I noticed a small pencil mark on the outer edge. I peered closer to see the number six scratched hastily into the wooden frame.

I backed away and stared at the number. Artists and curators were known to mark their paintings numerically or alphabetically for their own records but, whether this was done by Guillard himself or by the auction I could not tell. I also doubted it had anything to do with the thefts so I turned away from the painting and resumed my place at Mr. Langley's side, shaking my head slightly to indicate that I had noticed nothing out of the ordinary.

Already losing his patience with the impertinent Mr. Dabner and further hope dwindling at the knowledge that I had found nothing helpful from the painting itself, Mr. Langley sighed as I approached.

"Give all of your information to the detectives, Mr. Dabner. They will handle it from here," Mr. Langley said and the older man looked up at him then, eyes locking with my employer's' in a fierce rage.

"Weren't you supposed to have caught this man by now, Langley?" Mr. Dabner spat. "Perhaps they oversold your talents in America if a common art thief eludes you."

"I assure you, Mr. Dabner," Mr. Langley responded, calmer than I could have imagined but that hard edge to his voice still remained. "There is nothing common about this case."

With that, he took me by the arm and steered me out of Mr. Dabner's home and back to our awaiting carriage. I could tell, by the set of his brow and the tension of his jaw, that Mr. Langley was not pleased as he helped me into the carriage and then climbed in behind me. He thumped the top of the cab and the driver shot off at speed. We sat in silence for a few moments before I felt compelled to break it.

"We could still go to the police about the letter," I told him. "The handwriting analysis we've done. It could prevent another piece of artwork from being destroyed or stolen."

"It is not enough for the police to issue an arrest and I would rather Mr. Dubois not know that we are onto him," Mr. Langley said with a sigh, leaning back in the carriage and closing his eyes. I fell silent then, having felt a bit like I had been scolded, like my suggestion had been stupid. He must have sensed by unease because he opened his eyes and looked at me. They softened and he sat forward on his seat. "Besides, if he is as desperate as he appears to be for whatever is behind those paintings, closing in on him may only result in him going after more paintings, quicker, trying to get to whatever it is he needs before he's caught."

I nodded in understanding and turned my eyes to the road outside. I watched the people and houses that passed by for the remainder of our journey. Neither of us spoke again. That is, until we arrived at his house to find Bernard strolling swiftly from the door to the sidewalk to meet our carriage as it arrived, something he had never done before. Mr. Langley still took the time to help me from the carriage, though it appeared that something urgent was happening inside.

"Mr. Langley," Bernard said as he approached, there was a bit more uncertainty in his voice than I cared for. It set my teeth on edge. "It's- you have- there's a visitor."

"A visitor?" Mr. Langley asked, pleasantly enough though I imagined he noticed Bernard's anxiety as well. The butler's eyes shifted to me and that's all it took. I lifted my skirts and walked as quickly as I could to the door and into the house beyond. I heard the men's footsteps following close after me but they were out of my mind just as soon when I saw my youngest sister seated on the sofa in the drawing room. Her eyes were red and tears streamed down her cheeks. Miss Langley sat next to her, one arm around her shoulder in comfort. When she met my eyes, I saw the sorrow there. Not pity, not quite, but sorrow. I ran for my sister and came to a stop on my knees in front of her.

"Liza," I said, breathlessly, gripping her shoulders in my hands and forcing her to look at me. "Liza, what's wrong? Are you hurt?"

She shook her head and I felt a breath whoosh out of me in relief.

"I—It's father," she cried, breaking down into a fresh wave of tears as she did. "I can't find him! I only left the house for a second, Charlotte, just to get the newspaper, but Ben and Victoria were gone too and he- he just left! Charlotte, do you think he's-"

She stopped herself. Her eyes darted from me to Mr. Langley and back again, concerned that she was revealing too much, worried that I would not want my employer to know the misbehaviors of my family. She could not possibly know just how much he was aware of. I stood to my feet then and slid my gloves back on.

"Stay here Liza," I told her firmly. "I will return as soon as I'm able."

"You're going to get him?" she gazed up at me wide eyed but her gaze slipped back to Mr. Langley briefly. She could not admonish me for my willingness to go to such an inappropriate location with him present.

"I've been there once before," I reminded her. "I'll be just fine. Please. Stay here with Mr. and Miss Langley."

"If you think I am going to allow you to travel to a gambling den on your own, I'm afraid you don't know me well at all, Miss Porter," Mr. Langley said then in a slow drawl as he stepped in front of me, blocking my path to the door. I cast a glance over my shoulder to see Liza's open mouth and Miss Langley's eyes boring into my own, warning me not to challenge him on this. I sighed.

"Very well," I told him, pushing past him for the door. "Be quick about it then. Every moment we waste is another coin I'll have to pay."

Mr. Langley paused in surprise at my admission. I cursed myself for it in the moment. He had not quite known that I was personally paying my father's debts before. Perhaps he had suspected it but I had never confessed to the matter. Oh well. There was nothing to be done for it now. So I strode out of the front door and to the idling carriage. Harold had long since learned not to stay too far away from Mr. Langley and I unless Mr. Langley sent him off since we were always coming and going from one place to another. I approached him and gave him the address to the appropriate gambling hall and Mr. Langley arrived in time to help me into the carriage.

We said nothing as we rode to the seedier east end of London. Mr. Langley seemed to surmise, correctly, that I was in no mood for conversation. I was simmering quietly in my seat, angry with my father, angry at his addiction, and scolding myself for my anger all the while. He was a sick man who needed help not wrath. But I was near my breaking point with patience.

When we arrived, Mr. Langley and I left the carriage, telling Harold to linger close by, and made our way into the gambling hall. The greasy haired man behind the counter lifted his lip in a sneer as we approached.

"Miss Porter," he said in a sickly sweet condescension. "Come to pay upon your father's debts? I'm afraid you'll find the number has quite increased since our last meeting."

"Where is he?" I asked, taking great pains to keep the snarl from my voice. Greasy hair said nothing, only cast a lazy smile toward the opposite corner of the room. I turned to see my father's back facing me. He was hunched over a card table. His right hand was scratching his old scalp and his left was grasping a bottle. I sighed and pushed my way through the crowd toward him. Mr. Langley must have been following close at my heel the way the crowd parted around me but I hadn't noticed.

"Papa," I said, as gently as I could when I approached. My father turned to look at me and surprise registered upon his face but then slackened into sorrow. His eyes were glassed over and crazed and he swayed a bit even seated. Drunk, then. That would add an extra level of wonderful embarrassment to this evening. I placed a hand gently on his arm. "Papa, you scared Liza half to death. Come now, we need to get you home."

"I- but- I was about to play another game. I really think that this time, I've grasped the rules quite well so- It's American, you know. New to England and I think I could master it if-"

"Papa, please, it's late. Let's go."

He looked from me to the cards and then sighed. With a nod, he tossed down his cards and stood, leaning so heavily on my arm that I had to brace myself against the table to steady him. Mr. Langley was there in an instant, offering his other arm to help take the weight off of me. My father looked up at him and his lips opened to pose a question but he never got to ask it.

"Where do you think you're going, old man?" a deep rumble of a voice asked and I looked up to see the largest man I had ever seen. His bulging muscled arms crossed in front of his chest as he narrowed his beady eyes down at us.

"My father is finished," I told him with as much firm courage as I had within me while still holding up my aging father. "We are leaving."

"He's down quite a bit," the man told me then. "He either plays to raise it back up or we add it to his debt. It's up to you."

His lips curved into a wicked smile at that and I felt my temper rising. I stamped it down with a deep breath through my nostrils as I faced him.

"I suppose you will have to add it to his debt," I told him. "Take it out of the extra payment I gave you this week. He will play no more."

"That will bring your interest up as well, little Miss," he said rudely and my anger flared once more. "I'm not convinced you're good for it. Money may not be enough. You may have to resort to paying your father's debts by... other means."

His eyes flickered to my chest and I bristled but, before I could speak, I heard a chair squeaking beside me. I turned to see Mr. Langley settling into the seat that my father had previously occupied.

"Deal me in," he said calmly to the men at the table. "And step away from Miss Porter if you would like to keep violence out of your establishment tonight, sir."

The dealer looked up at the burly man in front of me. The man just nodded and the dealer began doling out the cards. I deposited my father on a nearby chair and returned to Mr. Langley's side.

"Mr. Langley," I said earnestly. "You don't have to do this. It's quite alright. I will make extra payments. My sister can part with some of her husband's profits. It isn't-"

"This game," he said, interrupting me. He then glanced past me to my father. "It's American, you say?"

My father nodded, stunned. "Poker, they call it."

Mr. Langley nodded and collected his hand. Then he spoke quietly under his breath so that only I could hear. "Stay close to me, Miss Porter, and I will see that no harm comes to you."

I could only nod, dumbstruck, and seat myself next to my father. I watched Mr. Langley as he played. He was calm and collected. Not a single shadow passed over his face as he played. His expression did not change a single time. There was no slight uptick of the mouth, no creasing of the brows, no wrinkling of the nose. His handsome face was completely devoid of the expressions I had come to know. He stared intently at all of his rival players, hardly glancing at his cards at all. He won the first round. Then the second. And the third. He won again and again until he broke precisely even on the debt that my father had accrued this very evening. Then he set down his cards and rose from his seat to face the burly man who was standing over him, red faced and angry.

"I have eliminated Mr. Porter's extra debt for the night," Mr. Langley told the man. "I do not seek to make a profit for myself, only to make it as though Mr. Porter never ventured in here this evening. I want no trouble and would like to be on my way with Mr. Porter and his daughter now. Do you intend to stop us?"

The man looked from Mr. Langley to us and grunted. Then he slid to the side so that we could pass. Mr. Langley helped me with my father as we led him out of the gambling den and into the waiting carriage outside. I nurtured my father the whole way back to Mr. Langley's home, trying to speak to him and sober him up, trying to ascertain if he had been threatened or hurt in any way. Mr. Langley said nothing but watched me care for him as we rode. When we arrived, Mr. Langley went inside to retrieve Liza and then rode with us as we took them back to the butcher shop. Victoria came running outside the moment we arrived.

"Papa! Liza! What happened?" she cried as she met us on the sidewalk. My father stumbled against Mr. Langley who kindly held him up. Victoria paled at the sight of him. "Papa, look at the state you're in! Benjamin!"

Benjamin came running from the shop and, seeing my father leaning against Mr. Langley, took him gently by the arm and took his entire weight as he led him carefully back into the shop and toward the stairs to the residence above. Liza followed after them, casting one sorrowful glance back at me as she went. She must feel terrible for having, what she considered to be, exposed the disfunction of my family to my gentleman employer. I would have to assure her later that she had done no harm. Victoria seemed to be thinking much along the same vein for she looked apologetically to Mr. Langley.

"I am so very sorry, Mr. Langley," she said, her cheeks flushing with embarrassment. "Oh, what you must think of us. Please, I do hope that it will not interfere with Charlotte's employment. She is truly a remarkable young woman and a hard worker and I will personally ensure that this does not happen again."

"Miss Porter is indeed remarkable," Mr. Langley said with a smile in my direction. "That fact is even clearer to me now that I see how deeply she cares for her father. How you all do."

Victoria smiled at that and looked to me. "Still, I feel as though I owe you a great debt, Mr. Langley. For saving our father tonight and for employing our dear Charlotte. We do not have much but if you would care to join us for dinner some night, you would be more than welcome."

I stared at my sister for a moment. Why would Mr. Langley, a man who could afford fine cuisine and servants to cook it, ever dine with my family in their modest, cramped apartment over a stinking butcher shop?

"I would be honored," Mr. Langley answered and my head snapped in his direction in surprise. "Say tomorrow evening?"

"Wonderful," my sister said with a smile and then turned to head back into her shop. "We will see you two then."

I turned my shocked expression on him but he only smiled and held out a hand to help me back into the carriage. I took it and waited for him to join me inside.

"You are full of surprises tonight, aren't you?" I said to him as Harold took off to take us home. He smiled at me. "Where did you learn to play poker like that?"

His smile faltered then and he turned his attention to the window and the dark streets beyond.

"I'm no stranger to the draw of the cards, Miss Porter," he said quietly and the carriage fell silent. I watched him in that silence. He was quite the puzzle to me. I had met my fair share of the rich and noble through my father's shop but had never met a gentleman whose personality to me seemed to be such an enigma. Every time that I thought I had figured the man out, he revealed another part of himself to me and I was left feeling as muddled as the day we had first met. He turned to me suddenly and smiled. "Perhaps I will tell you all about my time in America some day, Miss Porter. But tonight is not that night."

I nodded in understanding and did my best to push the clawing feeling of curiosity from my mind. We arrived back at Mr. Langley's home soon enough and made our way out of the carriage and into the house. Miss Langley was still awake and waiting. She stood from her spot in the drawing room as we entered. Her gaze passed by me and she met her brother's eyes. They engaged in that strange sibling communication which required no words for a brief moment before her eyes slid to mine.

"Charlotte," she said as she took a step forward. Her tone was sympathetic, concerned, but somehow lacking the pity that I had expected. She was not condescending, she did not speak to me as though I was fragile, but the shame was in my heart all the same and it warmed my face and brought moisture to the corners of my eyes.

"Thank you," I spat quickly, in an effort to stop any sweet, sympathetic words that she or her brother might speak. They had been kind enough as it was, far more understanding than any employer would be expected to be, and I could not allow them to commit any further kindnesses on my behalf. It had been an eventful evening and my emotions were utterly frayed. I could feel the tears coming already. I needed to excuse myself before they had the chance to fall so I rushed on ahead before either of them could speak a word more. "Both of you. I truly appreciate all you've done for my family this evening and I don't imagine I can ever repay you. But, if you don't mind too terribly, I'm rather exhausted and so I would like to excuse myself for the evening."

Elena's eyes shot to her brother again.

"Of course, Miss Porter," Mr. Langley said in answer to her unasked query. "Good night."

15 Solved

"Are you confident that you could remove the paintings from their frames without harming them?" Mr. Langley asked me over breakfast the next morning. I looked up from my plate of eggs to see him watching me. An assortment of case files and papers laid strewn about on the table in front of him. I nodded as I took another bite.

"It's similar in process to book binding", I told him. "My older sister Victoria spent some time one summer working on some canvases for an uptown art gallery and I helped her out some."

"Perhaps we should just go around collecting the paintings and seeing if there is anything hidden in the bindings."

"I don't imagine even you could convince those men to allow us to tamper with their priceless artwork in such a way", I told him. "But I do believe that if there was something behind the painting, we would be able to feel for it without removing the binding."

Mr. Langley nodded and stood. I sat my fork down and rose with him as he gathered his files and made his way for the door. I followed dutifully after, collecting my things from the awaiting Bernard and flashing him a smile before following Mr. Langley out of the house and into the carriage.

"That is precisely what we will do this morning, then", he told me as he helped me inside.

He meant it. We went house to house, requesting to feel behind the binding of each Guillard painting. Though the owners had many questions, they eventually acquiesced and allowed us to conduct our investigation. Mr. Langley allowed me to feel the binding myself, saying that I had more knowledge of the process and would be able to discern a difference far better than he could. So, for a majority of the morning, we drove house to house, inspecting each painting for a strange object in the binding which may or may not be there. I was beginning to doubt our theory of something of value being placed in the binding altogether by the time we returned to Mr. Langley's house for lunch. We entered the dining room and Mr. Langley tossed the papers onto the table before sitting in his seat and sighing. Elena was already there and halfway through her own bowl of soup.

"Difficult morning?" she asked with a quirk of the brow as we joined her and the servants placed two bowls of our own in front of us. I thanked Maggie as she curtsied and left us to our lunch.

"An unsuccessful morning", Mr. Langley answered, rubbing his cheek with a hand. He looked positively exhausted. I frowned and turned to eat my soup but then my eyes caught on a familiar sheet of paper. I reached out and grabbed it, pulling it closer. It was the list of buyers from the original auction. My eyes scanned the page and a realization dawned upon me.

"It's in order", I said suddenly and Mr. and Miss Langley both turned to look at me.

"Miss Porter?" Mr. Langley asked.

"The list. The thief is going down the list. In order. Look at this", I said, turning it around so he could see it. He leaned forward and read down the page, looking up at me, eyes wide in realization as he did.

"We took this directly from the treasurer's ledger", he said then and I knew he was thinking along the same lines as me. "It's the official auction list."

"Who else, besides the auction's treasurer, would have a copy of that list?"

Mr. Langley's eyes met mine and I knew that he understood what I was saying.

"The seller?" Miss Langley interjected but Mr. Langley's eyes did not leave mine.

"Look at who is next on the list", I said and he finally tore his eyes away from me to look back at the list in his hand.

"Mr. Herbert", he said and then we were both on our feet and heading for the door.

Miss Langley stood and called out to us in confusion but we were out of the door before I could quite hear what she had said. Mr. Langley helped me into the carriage and ordered the driver to head for the Herbert's house in haste. I felt restless on the ride, as if we were racing against something we didn't quite understand. When we arrived, Mr. Langley told Harold to wait and led me to the front door as quickly as he was able. The butler answered on the first knock and went swiftly to find Mr. Herbert when Mr. Langley indicated our urgency.

"Mr. Langley, Miss Porter", Mr. Herbert said a moment later, appearing in the foyer from a room beyond. "How lovely to see you both again. I hear that my wife and daughter have paid you a visit, Mr. Langley. They seemed utterly delighted to-"

"Yes", Mr. Langley interrupted the pleasantries. "They are lovely and always welcome in my home, of course. But, forgive me, Mr. Herbert, we are in a bit of a hurry. We've had a break in the case, you see, and we think that your remaining Guillard painting is next on the thief's agenda."

"Oh dear, what makes you say that?"

"It's a working theory. We have a few of them. One of which requires my partner here to feel the binding of your painting if you don't mind."

"Feel the binding... I'm sorry. I'm afraid I don't understand."

I pushed forward then, aware of the time we were wasting.

"Mr. Herbert, you know of my love of art as well as anyone. Do you believe that I would intentionally do harm to such a beautiful masterpiece?" I asked kindly but firmly. Mr. Herbert looked from my employer to me and his expression softened.

"Right this way, Miss Porter."

I cast a glance back at Mr. Langley as we followed after Mr. Herbert, back into the study in which we had first viewed the Guillard painting. It was hanging there still, untouched and as beautiful as ever. I approached it cautiously, gently pulling the frame away from the wall and feeling at the paper beneath. Mr. Herbert watched me carefully, dodging easily Mr. Langley's efforts to divert his attention from my actions with conversation. I felt the smooth paper beneath my fingers, pressing lightly until I felt the canvas beneath. I ran my fingers along the edges and froze. There, at the bottom, in the left corner, the paper raised. I felt the edge of something very thin, almost imperceptible. If I hadn't been searching for just this, I never would have noticed it. I looked to Mr. Langley who understood immediately what I had found.

"Mr. Herbert", he said quickly. "We believe there is a valuable piece of evidence hidden within your painting and we need to extract it."

"Evidence?" Mr. Herbert sputtered in surprised indignation. "Extract it? What are you-"

"I'll need proper tools", I told Mr. Langley then. "Mr. Young will have what I need."

Mr. Langley nodded in understanding. Of course the treasurer who sold paintings himself would likely have the tools needed to frame them.

"Mr. Herbert, we have to remove this painting from its frame and binding to extract what lies behind it. No harm will come to it. Miss Porter is a professional. If you will allow us to take it to Mr. Young's-"

"I'm coming with you", Mr. Herbert said then. "I'm not letting it out of my sight. Not while there's a Guillard thief about and not when you say mine is likely the next target."

Mr. Langley nodded and moved forward to help me remove the painting from the wall. Mr. Herbert helped as well after a moment when he recovered his manners from his surprise and knew better than to allow a woman to help carry such a heavy item. He and Mr. Langley took it carefully to the carriage and we all squeezed in as well. Mr. Herbert sat next to the painting while Mr. Langley and I sat together, pressed tightly together in the small space. I tried to ignore the uptick of my beating heart as Harold sped off toward Mr. Young's shop.

It was some time before we arrived and the gentlemen carried the painting into the shop. I followed after them, ensuring that they were careful.

"Gentlemen", I heard Mr. Young's voice exclaim as we entered the shop. "Mr. Langley, Mr. Herbert, a pleasure to see you both again and together no less. What do you have here? Miss Porter!"

He broke into a smile as he exclaimed my name and his eyes hooded at once, leaving no doubt in my mind that he entirely remembered our previous flirtatious encounter.

"Mr. Young", I said kindly in greeting. Though I did not care for the way his eyes roved over my body at my entrance, I knew that we needed the use of his tools and offending him would likely be a disadvantage.

"It's a pleasure to see you again, Miss", he said, his grin so wide it threatened to overtake him as he approached. He took my hand in his own and kissed it, lips lingering on my knuckles. Mr. Langley cleared his throat and Mr. Young turned to face him.

"We believe there is something hidden behind the binding of this painting and we would like to extract it but we lack the proper tools", Mr. Langley explained, getting straight to the point. "We thought that you may have them, Mr. Young."

"Indeed, I do", he said, leaving me to myself and approaching the painting, eyes roving over the artwork for the first time. "But I've no great skill in removing the binding, I'm afraid. I'm much better at the initial framing, myself. I would not want to risk such a feat on beautiful artwork such as this."

"We only have need of the tools", Mr. Langley explained further. "Miss Porter can remove the binding."

Mr. Young spun on his heels in surprise, eyes landing on me once more.

"Truly?" he asked, stunned. "You possess such a skill, Miss Porter?"

I nodded.

"Well, you're quite the delightful puzzle, aren't you?" he asked, a smile spreading over his lips again. Mr. Langley cleared his throat once more.

"The tools, Mr. Young?"

"Yes, I will return."

He left the room then and I approached the painting myself. Mr. Langley and Mr. Herbert had placed it flat upon a large oak table. I asked them to flip it over and they did. Then I removed my gloves and set them aside before running my finger along the edge to judge the binding. It had been poorly done, cheaply. The stitches were crooked and the frame was scratched. Whoever had gotten these framed initially had not taken them to someone very experienced in the work.

Mr. Young returned with the tools and I set to work without a word. It was a slow process since I was taking great care not to harm the valuable painting itself and because the work had been done so sloppily in the first place. I bent over my work, bringing my eyes as close to the painting as I could. I tried to ignore the sensation that someone was staring at my behind but could only do so for so long before I turned to see Mr. Young standing directly behind me. He cleared his throat and looked in another direction. I restrained the urge to roll my eyes as I reached into the frame. I was finished. I pulled gently and the binding fell away to reveal the canvas underneath.

There, nestled against the wooden bars, was a parchment of paper folded in half. Mr. Herbert gasped at the presence of the paper. I looked up at Mr. Langley who stepped forward and plucked it from the casing. He opened it and read, his eyes scanning the page. His lips parted in surprise as he read and then he passed it to me. I took it and read as well.

It was addressed to "Whomever Shall Find" it and was written in Vincent Guillard's own hand. In it, he explained that he chose to hide this letter in his favorite painting in the hopes that, should anything ever happen to him, someone would find it. He told the whole story, the years he worked on his incredible art, the day that he had met Mr. Dubois and they had formed an intense friendship from the start. He claimed that their relationship had progressed farther than the bonds of friendship and Mr. Guillard had fancied himself in love but then Mr. Dubois had begun to get paranoid, claiming that he was afraid people would find out about them and that it would ruin his status as a gentleman and endanger his inheritance as his father would never allow for him to inherit his family's fortune if such a scandal should break. But Mr. Guillard loved him and had believed the world would be accepting of them since they were so rich and talented with so many friends who already loved them. In the end, Mr. Dubois had begun to threaten him, to fear him and what he could reveal and, though they had since stopped seeing each other, Mr. Guillard was afraid that Mr. Dubois would try to harm him. So he hid this letter for investigators to find should that happen and left clues in his diary of its existence.

"Diary?" I asked aloud. Mr. Langley shook his head.

"It wasn't in the evidence collected from Mr. Guillard's studio", he told me.

"So Dubois must have it."

"Which means he is aware of this letter."

"So this is what he's been after."

I held the letter more closely at that. This was the evidence we had needed, the confirmation that we had been searching for which tied Mr. Louis Dubois to, not only the thefts but to a homicide that had been framed to look like a suicide.

"Thank you, Mr. Young, Mr. Herbert," Mr. Langley said then. He reached into his pocket and pulled out some coins. He handed them to Mr. Young. "Mr. Young, please rebind this painting for Mr. Herbert. Mr. Herbert, I will have a constable sent to your home to help protect it until our suspect is in custody. Thank you both for your assistance."

Then Mr. Langley pushed past them both and, taking my arm in his, lead me out of the shop and back to the carriage. When we arrived, he told Harold to hurry to the police station and hurry he did. I had to hold onto the seat to avoid being pitched into the floor of the carriage. Mr. Langley reached out to steady me on more than one occasion. When the carriage pulled up to the curb outside of the station, Mr. Langley and I were out of it and rushing up to the door in an instant.

"Good afternoon Mr. Langley. How may I-"

But Mr. Langley did not wait for the desk sergeant to finish his question. He breezed right past him and into the station, pulling me along behind him. I practically jogged to keep up with his long strides as he barged into Chief Detective Ryland's office and threw the letter down atop the surprised officer's desk. Ryland looked to the paper and up to Mr. Langley and I, eyebrow quirked with interest.

"Get your men and go arrest Louis Dubois," Mr. Langley spoke in a hurried tone but the Chief Detective just leaned back in his chair and narrowed his eyes in examination of the gentleman.

"On what charge?"

"Breaking and entering, theft, unlawful sale of stolen property," Mr. Langley rattled off the list with some intensity but the Chief Detective's expression did not change until he had voiced the last. "And murder."

"Murder."

"Yes. Murder."

"Who exactly was Mr. Dubois supposed to have murdered?"

"His lover, Vincent Guillard."

In that moment I wished that Vincent Guillard was alive or some such painter had been present for they may have been able to immortalize the shocked expression upon the Chief Detective's face.

"His... lover?"

"It's all in the letter. And what isn't, is in the ledgers."

"What ledgers?"

"The ledgers which are currently in the possession of a Mr. Young. I am certain that if you made the request, he would part with the pages in question."

"I see," The Chief Detective rose to his feet slowly, staring down at the folded parchment with newfound interest. He reached forward, grabbed the stationary, and tucked it neatly away in his breast pocket before clearing his throat and crossing the room behind us to the door on the opposite side. "Well then. I will take Detectives York and Higgins with me to make the arrest. Perhaps they can explain to me along the way precisely why they were so quick to rule Mr. Guillard's death a suicide."

"Detective Ryland," Mr. Langley spoke and the Chief Detective halted at the door, hand on the doorknob, slightly annoyed by the lack of his full title in the address. "Our discovery of Mr. Guillard's death being, in fact, a homicide came from a tip from one of your own officers. I'd like to ensure he gets some recognition for his excellent observational skills but does not have to fear retribution from his superiors."

I found myself smiling at Mr. Langley, pleased that he had remembered the boy. If he noticed my satisfaction, he made no show of it.

"Which officer?" the Chief Detective asked.

"Officer Umber."

The Chief hesitated a moment but then nodded curtly, opened his door, and left his office. Mr. Langley turned to me then and smiled, having noticed my own beaming back at him.

"What?" He asked, genuinely curious. But I could not bring myself to admit my own admiration.

"What do we do now?" I asked.

"We wait."

"Here?"

"Yes, indeed. I do not count my cases closed until I've seen the man locked away myself.

I nodded and took a seat in one of the chairs in front of the Chief Detective's desk, pleased with our work.

"I do feel for him though," I said then and Mr. Langley looked up at me in surprise.

"For the murderer?" he asked and I winced at the judgement in his tone.

"There is no excuse for murder," I began so that he knew my feelings on the matter clearly enough. "But as for the motive. He was so afraid to love who he loved, so terrified to be himself, that he would resort to such a terrible thing."

Mr. Langley watched me curiously.

"Our society has quite a few rules about love," he said finally though his feelings on such a statement were not clear by the making of it. "But homicide is homicide. The police will speak to Mr. Dubois about the letter and I have no doubt they will reach a resolution. Mr. Dubois strikes me as the kind of man to confess."

I nodded. I agreed with that sentiment at least. I sat quietly for a moment, staring down at my frayed gloves, picking at the little strings frayed at the seams. I should feel proud. I should feel accomplished. I had solved my first case with Mr. Langley. But, in truth, I found myself feeling surprisingly unhappy that it was over and excited for the one that would follow.

We remained in the Chief Detective's office for some time, me fidgeting with my gloves and Mr. Langley watching the bustle of the busy police station beyond the Chief Detective's windows. Finally, after what felt like an eternity, a commotion sounded from the front of the building. Someone was shouting and a familiar voice boomed back at them.

"-can meet with your attorney the moment we can get a hold of him," The Chief Detective was saying as the doors of the station were opened for him and he and his two leading detectives made their way into the station, Mr. Dubois in handcuffs between them. As they led him past, he turned and saw Mr. Langley and I standing there, in the Chief Detective's office, and I felt a chill run down my spine. Not because of the sneer he cast in our direction. Not because of the anger that seemed to be radiating off of him in waves. Not even because of the way he was shouting and ranting that they couldn't treat him like this. What rooted me to my spot and stopped my breathing was his hat. A very familiar, perfectly circular, bowler hat. My mouth popped open in surprise.

"Miss Porter?" Mr. Langley asked, concerned. I managed to shake away my shock enough to smile sheepishly up to my employer.

"I've just... never seen anyone arrested before," I lied. He nodded.

"Mr. Langley," Chief Detective Ryland called out, returning to his office as his detectives found their desks and tossed the criminal onto a chair between them to begin their processing. "We've got some paperwork to complete now that this business is over, of course. Come with me?"

Mr. Langley nodded and turned to follow the Chief Detective. I did not. Rather, I remained firmly rooted to the spot, staring at Louis Dubois who now sat, agitated, as Detectives York and Higgins leered over him, mocking him for his capture.

"Miss Porter?" He called out once more out of concern.

"I think I will remain here," I responded. "If you do not mind. I may go for some fresh air."

Mr. Langley hesitated but ultimately nodded and followed the Chief Detective into his office, closing the door tightly behind them. I watched as the Detectives worked through the paperwork on Mr. Dubois' case, listened as they teased him, relaxing with their hands behind their heads, leaning back in their chair and knowing that he could do no such thing. He was glaring at them but he was no longer shouting. Some of the fight seemed to have left him after his grand entrance.

After a few minutes, the Detectives got up and, laughing, made their way toward the back rooms, toward the evidence which needed recording in Mr. Dubois' case. I seized the moment and approached him. Handcuffed and unable to move, he didn't seem so sinister. But when he looked up at me and our eyes met, I saw who he was hidden behind them. A murderer. He killed his lover and he might have killed me too that night on the dark, uninhabited London streets.

"Was it you?" I asked. I had meant for the question to come out as a demand for information but it came out far quieter and far more timid than I had hoped.

"I don't have any idea what you're talking about," He lied. I could tell by his smirk.

"Did you follow me? That night. From my family's shop?"

Detectives York and Higgins were returning. I saw them reenter the room from behind him. Still, I kept my eyes firmly locked on Dubois so that I did not miss it when his expression changed and he smiled broadly up at me.

"You have secrets that no one knows, Miss Porter," he told me, a mischievous glint in his wicked eyes. "Not even your beloved employer."

Before I could respond, the detectives were hoisting him from the chair, admonishing him for speaking to me, and dragging him off to a holding cell to await his trial. He did not seem to mind. That horrible smile remained on his face and his eyes remained on mine even as they led him away. I watched him as well, unable to look away, unable to shake the feeling of dread that his cryptic words had brought upon me. A woman who had no secrets, someone who had nothing to fear, would have shaken off Mr. Dubois' strange warning as nothing more than a trick. But, then again, was there truly any woman without her secrets? So, despite my best efforts to appear stronger than I was, I was left wondering what precisely Mr. Dubois had meant. And what it was that he knew.

"Miss Porter?" Someone asked and I spun around to see Mr. Langley standing behind me, head cocked curiously to one side.

"Mr. Langley!" I exclaimed, all too eagerly. "All finished then?"

He hesitated. He seemed to be weighing the possible outcomes of questioning what had occurred between Dubois and myself but must have decided against it for he simply held his arm out for me to take and nodded.

"What's next?" I asked then, looping my arm through his own and looking up into his eyes. He smiled at me. He must have seen the eagerness there.

"Dinner with your family," he said and I sighed, slumping back into my seat. He smiled. "Tonight, remember?"

"I do."

His eyes met mine and did not break away. The smile on his lips was different somehow and the look in his eyes was one that I could not place. I opened my mouth to ask him what he was thinking when something caught my eye from outside of the curtain and I looked to find that we were not on our way back to Mr. Langley's superior part of town but were in a rather different area indeed.

"The East End," I said in surprise. "Mr. Langley, where are we-"

"Our investigation into the matter of the Guillard Art Thief is complete," Mr. Langley told me, nodding his head in the direction of a familiar look-ing gambling den as we approached it. "Now we can focus our attentions on the investigation of far more importance to us both."

THE END.

www.ingramcontent.com/pod-product-compliance
Lightning Source LLC
Chambersburg PA
CBHW070350200726
48294CB00003B/831